PAUL JOHN ADAMS

METARULES OF THE S·M·F

OPTIONAL BOOKS

Metarules of the S·M·F

1.

GUESS I BEEN PRETTY WILD from a young age without much excuse.

My brother Rhad disappeared when he was six and I was five. I barely remember him, but I feel a kind of sickness when I think of his absence. It's not something you can describe. I remember competing with him, scrapping one time, with our mom shouting. I don't know. It's sad the only strong memory I have is a fight. And some of the bad feeling in the family after that, between me and my mom—it just became a fact I couldn't do nothing about—a part of the fabric.

Materially, though... I guess I got treated fair enough. Mom was good to me, there was no drug use in the family, and I went to a decent elementary school. I ate well, Mom cleaned the house, she did her best to keep me straight.

And at night I sometimes talk to... I don't know, I just talk... hoping Rhad is with my father somewhere. But he probably dead.

But you don't want to know the kind of lives my S·M·F brothers went through in they youth. And like I said, family shit don't affect me much because I hardly remember it. Just indirectly, you know?

My mom was a real hard-ass, and she did everything she could to keep me from associating with the wrong kind of kids. There really wasn't many *wrong-kind-of* kids at my age when we were young, but there were some teenagers up to some bad business up in Staircase Alley, and I wasn't supposed to talk to them, and I didn't. Looking back, they were probably just a bunch of fuck-ups bored out they mind.

We lived in a little finger of a black neighborhood that extended a few blocks south of Silver Avenue, whereas most of the stupid shit and criminal activity went on north of there. Our neighborhood centered on the two parallel streets of Ducasse and Thomas, and I made friends with some of the boys on Dorsey, running down from Silver Ave to Pearl Street. I was a "Duckis" kid, and proud of it. Some humans in our area had the pretention to think we were upclass to Jack-Rabbit Corner. True, there was more garbage on they streets, and more condemned houses. But we didn't have much to boast about.

Besides them, there was a buffer zone of weak-ass Latin punks lived between us blacks and the working class whites south of Yost. This was before shit heated up with the Walden Street Boys. We were supposed to feel proud of being part of the Brehms neighborhood school district, but Jack-Rabbit kids went there too, so it's not like it was selective.

◈

I first met Jonas Dandridge—to speak—in class. We done seen each other on the street a couple times, just passing, but I didn't really know him though he lived a block and a half up with his grandma. Guess he'd just moved in and hadn't hooked up with any friends on the street yet. The moms weren't eager to introduce us because his grandma was a addict. Not like she was the only one.

We didn't talk much at first, but then we got to talking about silly shit—cartoons mostly. We were nine then. Soon he was cracking jokes all the time, and he also talked a lot about sports, but not with me; I didn't know much about sports. Never cared at the time.

◈

When we came to kind of think of each other as friends, Dandridge was playing this ridiculous little hustle. He sold kids in our school a "present" for a quarter. What he called a "present" was a *secret gift* tightly wrapped in aluminum foil. When you paid for it, you got to open it and find out what you got. Every single time it was a nickel. Every time. It was ridiculous funny, and for kids who weren't in on the joke yet there was something tempting and mysterious about not knowing what you'd get. But while we were laughing about it, Dandridge was making money that added up. Eventually everyone caught on there was nothing to win but a nickel, and it cost you a quarter, so no one would buy the "presents" no more.

Dandridge took me aside and said, "Mala, here's what you gotta do. I'm going to offer you to buy a present, and when you open it up, it's going to be a dollar. It'll blow kids' minds. Then I'm back in business. So you keep your end, okay?"

It sounded cool, so when we were on the playground, Dandridge tried to sell me a "present," and I acted all coy and resistant, but then I said "Why not?" and I paid him my quarter and opened it up... and it was a nickel!

The kids laughed they asses off, but I was pissed. I shoved Dandridge back and said, "Hey, you told me..." and then he punched two or three times and I was down before I knew what was happening.

"Don't renege, bitch," he told me. Then he clonked me on the head with a rock.

This is not the first or last time you're going to hear about me getting hit with a rock neither. Clonks are like a common experience for me.

But I meant to tell you earlier, but I forgot, that Jonas Dandridge later became a great man and this whole book is about him. He later came to be known as "Cloud."

This white kid, Pete, when he saw us scrapping, "*Lizards* always fighting," he said. Well... what he really said was "*niggers.*" I don't like to spell it out; it don't normally fit with my philosophy to talk that way, but I guess to be honest I gotta report the way it was.

Humans think blacks always bringing ruckus, but it's

not like that at all. We tolerate a lot more shit than we really ought to, and we tolerated Pete as long as he was tolerable. When he was out of line, we shouted him down, and one time I knocked him down in the hall, but we didn't take it further. No one had yet taught us to be dignified enough we would make sacrifices to win respect. That would come later.

Generally though, racist shit didn't fly in that school most of the time because the teachers were progressive, and I got on quite well with most whites. Just not fucking Pete. And, believe it or not, I got on well with whites up to and including my time in juvie, which came in seventh grade. I was the first of my friends to be incarcerated.

2.

I WAS TWELVE when I had to stab this Afro named Doug. I took a big kitchen knife into school and stabbed him square in the back during social studies class, right out in front of everyone. That got me some three years locked up. It was a pretty stupid stunt, looking back on it. And those were pivotal years when a lot of stuff was going on, the kids were growing up, and the kids I'd rode bikes with and shared comic books with were starting to become a recognized force. Dandridge and I were already tight, and between us and our friends Thayne, Rick Pettis, and Daran Jackson, there was about five of us were really close, plus we had our associates. When I was down, I missed most of the big events when the boys were starting to organize the click, and Kevin Carter got involved—I didn't know him yet. They ran some Black Steel Nines out of Staircase Alley, and they also fought the tunnel wars to get access to the Yost Street underpass. They were just out to fuck around and run some raids and scrap in Boulevards territory, but I missed all the action.

Juvie was fucked up in many ways, but then, looking from another perspective, it was just like a school you never could leave. Cash was contraband, but we had some. The first few weeks seemed like forever. There were some clicks, but it was mostly disorganized. Walnuts ran the show. One kid got whipped into a coma by five guys with padlocks tied into the end of they socks. I could tell you a thousand stories about those first few weeks, but I won't waste your time.

The first advice I got was from a car thief, Efrem Bostic:

"You're stupid, man. You should've stabbed that kid in the ass-muscle. I'm serious. You stick a guy in the ass-muscle, it hurts like hell, he can't walk. But you acted in a conspicuous manner. Try to kill a kid right out in front of everyone, the teacher too. That's brazen. You get respect, but the authorities can't ignore. You gotta do time for that."

This sage advice was practical minded, but Efrem hadn't been wise enough to avoid getting hisself locked up neither. Within a few weeks of my arrival, he turned into a real good friend. I also befriended Kenneth Branch—known as "Fierce"— early on. He taught me a lot and was a real help. He especially helped me pick up gambling skills, whereas Efrem had less to teach me about the inside life—but his car knowledge became critical later, and he was just a cool guy, so we all got on well.

I didn't know much about gambling when I went in, and eventually I was like the second- or third-best tonk player—but I had to contend with a lot of cheats, and the black players were generally pretty savvy so I couldn't get much edge. I did hustle some money in it. I tried to formulate a strategy quickly, beyond the tips Fierce gave me. I was studying my math pretty seriously at that time, so I figured I could get an edge by analyzing the game, but the best players had psychology, knowledge, and grit on they side. Initially I just crunched numbers to find the right scores to drop at, against one, two, or three opponents. Nobody had done the math. I found most humans were too conservative about dropping. Actually, I tried to formulate a separate strategy to use against early-droppers and late-droppers, and ways to deal with sandbaggers, but it was a wasted effort. There was almost no early-droppers but me. At the same time, sandbagging wasn't too common, and it was used almost exclusively against me! They had instinct to know I was more trappable, so the couple of more cagey players forced a conservative dropping strategy, closing the gap and reducing my edge to a small margin. I still had some margin. But as I matured into the game, I became more of a psychology player and couldn't go with the numbers so much... or not exclusively.

The times when the money was easier was when the new kids joined who couldn't learn as quick as I. They dropped stupid and played drunk a lot. Some of them weren't concerned with winning, they knew they were born to lose, but they wanted to hang with us because we card players could be seen as a kind of click. We didn't really stand up for the weaker ones, but they had this perception hanging with us was safer—and at the same time a little more thrilling—than being alone. They were naïve, in other words.

But my main advantage was in the poker games with the white kids. I could play most games decent, and I mastered eight-or-better hi-lo stud. The players there were so pathetic, it was real easy to destroy they games, even when they made some clumsy efforts to cheat.

Unfortunately, one kid pushed me into a situation where I had to use some violence. When I went to the pictures, I found some marked cards he'd just had in his hand, and I couldn't ignore it. My prestige for being assaultor was on the line. White kid could fight too, and it was threatening to get racial when some of his friends chanted "whip the nigger." I don't want to brag because I don't got much to brag on, but luck was on my side, besides the fact I was a bit dynamic. We were swinging wild, and I had a fear his boys were going to get involved if I didn't resolve it quick, and while he was landing some blows, I made a wild swing that just went way off the mark, but I was leaning into it, off-balance, really reckless, when he came forward at a low and odd angle... put hisself right in my path so I didn't expect it when my left forearm smacked him. Then I pulled down to blast him with a right and struck hard on the side of his face, and his weak counterpunch didn't faze me, and he stumbled back a bit. Because he was inattentive, I got him backed into the wall and broke up the bones in his face pretty good. Afterwards I was surprised to find his teeth had cut my hand and elbow.

After I settled into the culture of the place, I don't know what happened. Time seemed to drag, but then, in retrospect, the time just went. There was a lot of... bad mood in there. But it was all so fucking tedious, and then the time just went. Sometimes I thought I'd die in there. It was outrageous. Three fucking precious years, man.

In that time I went from hustling potato chips to earning $659. Not much salary for three years of life. But coming to my last months, I made a prop bet for $400 getting $1200, faded by several of the other rich kids. I bet that out of the next 30 kids to arrive, two of them would have the same birthday. I was really a 7 to 3 favorite to win this bet, getting 3 to 1, which means 180% expected ROI. Pure murder in gambling terms, but some of those kids, for all they smarts, were just dumb at math, man. I took full advantage, though I could have got unlucky. Turned out kid number nine and kid fourteen both had the same birthday: July sixth. So then I got paid, and then I had well over eighteen hundred bucks. And then I was out.

3.

IN MY THREE YEARS DOWN, you could say I had a lot of time for soul-searching, but I didn't find anything in my search. Pretty much I felt I'd been cheated by life. And when I got released, I was locked out of my house. My mom didn't want anything to do with me. I think she was scared I'd been transformed into some kind of monster. We didn't have a big scene, but it was heartbreaking really.

She hadn't answered my calls for a while, and she knew release time was coming. But I thought she wouldn't turn me down when I came straight to the door. It's childish, but I thought when I got there, she'd just throw the door open and be overjoyed and cry tears of happiness to take me back, knowing I'm a good son who'd just done something stupid once and paid for it. But on another level, I knew that was a scene from another kid's life—probably a white kid's life—and this wasn't going to happen for me.

What really happened was I knocked at the door and there was no answer. Then I knocked harder and waited. And I said, "Mom, let me in."

Mom came near the inside of the door and said, "Don't you come here. I don't want to see you."

"Come on, Mom!"

"I'm not opening the door."

I felt pretty enraged to the point of wanting to burst, but I didn't want to disturb the neighbors. She'd be justified in rejecting me if I made a big scene. I wasn't having that. I just left. But, *Oh, my God, does she not even know!?* It's sad, really, we can't just figure things out and find a way to make things right when they wrong.

To tell the truth, I didn't know what to do or where to turn. I just wanted to get fucked up.

I walked across the ocean into the Wild Zone and bought me a half-quart of Country Club to drink while I just walked around wild-eyed and thinking about things. *Half the mother-fuckers I know who do wrong, no matter how bad they are, they moms stand by them. The other fuckers' moms no good. But my Mom's a good woman, and she won't have anything to do with me now? In a time of crisis? Unheard of. I must be the worst motherfucker there is.*

Meanwhile, there was a lot of kids out, it was an active night, but no one brought me any trouble.

Then I worked my way over into some really unfamiliar territory. Someone threw up a sign while I was passing, but I ignored it. Then walked back to the "safe side," down Thornlie, and threw my empty can at a Puerto-Rican window. Then circled back around. I avoided coming in sight of my mom's apartment again, and I thought maybe I should drop in on Jonas or Rick. But it was late, and none of the boys had bothered to visit me for the last eight months, so why was I going to bring my troubles to them right now? Kept on hoofing it to the seediest—the filthiest—part of Jack-Rabbit corner—and just threw myself down on the ground in an empty field full of weeds and junk.

"The problem is," I said to myself and to the moon, "I've been living a structured life. I don't know what to do without a prefab plan. I don't know what those other thugs do, but I never had it in my mind to live this kind of life at all. Fucking three years of posturing, man, just fake, I'm no gangster, I'm not even a criminal, not by choice. Things just happened, man, I mean what do they want from me now, huh? I was supposed to get me a big fat juicy steak when I came out. I got money, and the dream been with me for a long time; I could be downtown partying man, but I'm wallowing. This is just the definition of self-inflicted misery. I could be having sex right now, but the thought of those Jack-Rabbit hoes just sickens me. I didn't even drink enough to get buzzed, and I got enough jerking-off inside. I'm limp, man, fucking limp. But I'm just psyching myself, time to break the spell, man. I'm not going to wind up telling this pathetic tale to the boys inside. If I do get locked up again, I'll have to tell the same kind of bullshit story those other fags tell about they sexual conquests, bouncing tits and shit. But I'm better than that, man."

Then I fell asleep.

Clonk!

I didn't even know what was up when I scrambled up on all-fours and watched the confusing sight of my own blood pouring down onto the ground and splashing my face and shirt.

"Hnnnnnh."

Shaking my head, I splashed that blood like a dog. But I got my bearings. Some bastards were chunking rocks at my head while I slept, and it came to this.

"Homeless bitch! Get on up out our lot!"

I saw four of them, a little smaller than me individually. Then I went berserk. I picked up a stone with heft and threw that fucker right in the face of the one who'd called me "bitch"—I think. It caught him full force in the jaw and knocked him cold. A high-pitched gasp escaped his smashed-in mouth when his tailbone struck the pavement, but after that he barely wriggled, as I hurdled over him, only now aware that I was running—and I stopped. The three other boys were gone in three directions.

Scared of me? Huh. This is a strange world.

And they'd left they boy behind.

Two of the others stopped running when they were about eighty yards out. The third ran a little farther. And they watched.

I rolled the knocked-out sucker over, facedown, and stood by his feet, then picked up his ankles with him laid out behind me like a wheelbarrow. I dragged him around the street a bit to get out my anger. Then I let his legs fall and walked away.

And they scared of me? Very strange.

I didn't run until I was out of they sight. Then, when I got around the corner from Freya onto Crystal, I ran a few blocks then hiked over to Brandywine Park. There was some kids dicing. I decided to see who I could spook with my blood-face. I was kind of out of it.

"Whoah, shit!"

One guy was surprised. Then another, bigger kid came over to intercept me. He was built, too.

"Yo, don't fuck around here, kid, what's your problem?"

A voice called out, "Hold up!"

I looked and saw Jonas emerge from the crowd of unfamiliar faces... and then I saw a couple of others I knew too. Thayne was there.

"Malapha! What's going on?" said Jonas. "When'd you come out?"

"Today. Or yesterday. I don't know what day it is."

"Technically it's tomorrow, but hey, the sun's not up."

And Jonas grabbed me for a hug, and it was surprising to discover the years hadn't distanced us as much as I'd supposed. I felt alright.

Some of the boys went back to gambling while Jonas and a couple of the other guys got me to sit down on the pavement. Thayne looked as brooding as ever.

"What up, Thayne?"

"I'm alright. What happened to you?"

Jonas pushed his hand hard on my scalp.

"Ow."

"Hey," the big guy complained—this was the guy who'd blocked me out at first—"don't bloody my pants."

"It's not like it would be the first time," said Jonas.

"That's just the point. Who you think is paying for these jeans all the time?"

"Who the fuck are you!?" I shouted.

"Hush Mala. Sit still. This is Duane, and he's one of the boys, so chill. What happened?"

"I scrapped with some fuckers in the Corner."

"How many fuckers?"

"Four."

"And they cut you?"

Jonas took his hand off my head and shook off some of the blood from his palm, then cleaned his hand on the leg of Duane's pants.

"Hey, fuck you!"

"Ha, ha! I'll buy you new ones."

"You don't gotta do that, just don't fuck around, man."

"Nobody cut me. I got hit with a rock."

"Probably Baby-Man bitches. Nothing to worry about. Want to play See-Low?"

I cleaned my face and hands with my already ruined shirt, and got up with some assistance. Jonas had stopped the bleeding.

"Dizzy?"

"Not much."

Thayne slapped my back. Lettuce too.

"What up, Malapha, you doing alright?"

"Sure, sure."

"Hey, Mala's out!" Jonas announced to the rest of the click as he ushered me into the circle.

"We figured that much. Now put up or shut up, I'm thirty bucks in the hole already."

I pulled some money out my pocket to dice, and Jonas looked surprised at the knot.

"Damn. How much money you got on your first day out?"

"I got it inside."

"Damn. I need to get myself locked up!"

I spent the rest of the night until just before dawn picking up an extra fifty-five dollars, and I got acquainted with the boys

I didn't know and reacquainted with the ones I did. Thayne told me he missed me, and he looked sincere. Then I met the notorious Kevin Carter, who was profoundly drunk, lying flat on his back on the pavement but still conscious.

"Hey, man, don't step over me. Step around me."

"I wasn't going to step over you."

"You step over me, you inherit my dark energies. They fuck you up. They fuck you up, you don't want that. It's like what King Large said about *dark energies*, you know? Hey. Hey, check this out." He took a ring out his pocket, placed it on his nose, and closed his eyes. "This ring is gold, man, I'm telling you. I'm going to sleep now. You think someone'll take it?"

Lettuce quick snatched it off his nose and several of us laughed, but Kevin went on rambling.

"You don't want that, I'm telling you."

There was a lot of boys there, too, who were kind of outside the click, acting a little uncomfortable, or clustering in they own little groups that came and went, mostly losing some money, and a lot of kids were just bullshitting around the park, drinking. A lot of them looked at me, curious.

At dawn, I went back to my mom again, and this time she opened the door to me.

"Come in, Malapha. I'm sorry, but you know, it hurt me when you went away. So much, you don't know…"

So I got my homecoming after all, but Mom's change of heart came a little too slow for my liking.

4.

"YOU KNEW I wasn't going to forget you, Mala, right?" This was Jonas, the next day.

"Sure. But, you know, forgetting is one thing..."

"Let's go to the beach."

"What?"

"Shit. You don't know anything. Come on, I'll show you. There's a place out on the piers I like to go. Come on, Sammy!"

It was a thirty-minute hike through the white part of South Brehms, including a short jog down the industrial tracks and a hop over a fence to get to the disused pier. Jonas and I were accompanied by Sammy Benjamin. The rest of the kids got up to they own business.

We smoked bats at the end of the pier. Sammy had kept his mouth shut till now, and he seemed nearly morose.

"This is the ugliest damn 'beach' I ever seen," I said.

"Heh. True."

"So, what I miss?"

"Eh. Everything really. But nothing serious. We had a lot of fun, but I got a feeling it's time to get more serious. You know I'm going to be sixteen."

"Old timer."

"Serious Mother Fucker," said Sammy, speaking for the first time. "I'm serious, that's what we gotta call our click: the Serious Mother Fuckers."

"We talked about that. It's being considered." Then turning to me: "But, we gotta weed out the suckers, and I need to know if you met any hardcore types—but thinking types. You know, someone to build our strength, but reliable, not weak-headed."

"Sure, sure. I know two guys. Efrem will be out at the end of the month. I wanted to introduce him to you."

"Why can we trust him?"

"He's solid."

"Not psycho like you Mala?" asked Sammy and stuck his finger in his nose. "Because, prison, that's where you find dependable humans, right? Fucking nuthouse."

I half leaped up, and Sammy scrambled to his feet, backpedaling in an exaggerated mockery of panic.

"Oh my God, he's going to prove me wrong by throwing me in the river! That'll show how sane and dependable this cocksucker really is, right!?"

"What the fuck is wrong with you?"

"Cocksucker, cocksucker!"

Jonas was laughing his ass off. I looked at him, trying to figure the situation—what was really going on.

"What would you do?"

Jonas threw up his hands.

"Sammy's like that."

I decided to sit back down next to Jonas and ignore Sammy. I didn't know if that made me weak, or sane.

"I want to meet your guys," said Jonas. "Especially if they can help us make some money. But they can't do any kind of drugs. We don't tolerate that."

"When'd you get so straightlace?"

"I always been straightlace."

"I wouldn't say that."

"I might have been mean, and I might have done some shit, but that don't mean I can't have my principles. You know, I got a mind to make a nice place here for humans to live and prosper, with respect. We don't have to go the way of those other degenerate fuckers. They eat they own."

Sammy started pantomiming a man eating something—I think it was a baby because he rocked it a few times between taking bites.

"There's a lot of talk about you, Jonas. Humans saying you showed a lot of strength lately, especially in the Staircase-Alley Wars."

"That some crazy shit, man. Humans tell me I was crazy, I was going to die. But really it was like a game of tag with knives and bats. Hooks on they side. I organized the first raid, there was five of us, and we chased them out. We caught two, cut up they faces and bashed them up a bit. They came back a few weeks later, Nines, new soldiers. Well armed. We tried to run them out but they pulled, shot, and scattered us. But we were back. They came and went. Probably the fifth time we went out there, I got shot in the leg and this other kid, not in our click but just someone in the area, he got shot, but he recovered. We've pulled him in and now he's in. Isaac Damond. We call him *Young*, but he's growing fast. Meanwhile, we already started putting pressure on the Nines' business. It was the local law, no druggies buy from the alley. We threatened them with dire consequences, rape, all kinds of shit. Consequence, they started shopping elsewhere, and the Jack-Rabbit Fams picked up most of the business. I'd like to run all the druggies out of town completely, but you know, one step at a time."

"What about your grandma?"

"She moved to Florida, man, she living with my grandaunt."

"So where you live?"

"In my house."

"How you pay rent?"

"No rent. Grandma own it."

"So she just gives it to you?"

"Come on, man. For all the damage she done to the whole damn clan, least she can do is ensure one member is housed. So, yeah, it's my place. That's it."

"Sorry, sorry, tell the rest."

"Well… so, the Nines stopped camping where we always knew we could catch them, and they started running punitive raids of they own. One time they run in of a sudden with like fifty, sixty guys, knocked some of us around a bit. But even losing that skirmish, it was kind of a victory because they gave up the block. Some guys got hurt, I admit. Carter got his foot broke, and some other kids running with us, they got hurt. But it wasn't really worth that much to the Nines anyway, and next thing happened was the Indian guy who run Shazaam Liquors, you know, which was backed by Staircase, he was so fed up with the lost business due to the warring that he started cooperating with the police. So the Nines killed him, and that was that.

"I posted guys in the alley for some time. Then we just checked in once in a while. There hasn't been any trouble since. The talk was the Nines were going to kidnap me or some shit, but that never happened. They got other fish to fry. You know, they leadership changed. Los Asesinos captured and tortured Ruddy Biv, and the Family Of Man is encroaching. There's been kids dying up there every week for the last six months. But I got reputation and I'm cleaning up the neighborhood pretty good. You will *not* hear any complaints about me from kids, from adults, from authorities—except a few who got hurt in the early skirmishes—because I'm not bringing any bad influences into the community. I'm running them out."

"That's cool."

"Damn straight," said Sammy.

I smoked and pondered. I wanted to say something, but my ideas weren't really coming together, so I just improvised and it turned kind of messy.

"You know," I said, "I got this buzz lately."

"Why not?"

"What do you mean?"

"Why not?"

"Yeah, you'd think it's because I just got my freedom, but it goes beyond that. I just got this sense of urgency, you know. I can't live a mainstream life."

"Like you even got that option," said Sammy.

"Everyone's got they struggle," said Jonas.

"There's struggle, true, but I'm not going to strive and get nowhere. I don't see that happening."

"Where you want to go?"

"Good question. *Think about where you want to go before you go there.* That's idealistic, right?"

"Wrongheaded," said Sammy.

"You know what I'm saying. When I'm in a spot, I just feel like, *Where I want to go is not here.*"

"Sure."

"You're not the first to think that, though," said Jonas.

"Did you think that, Sammy?"

"I never thought a damn thing."

"Well, anyway..." I brought it back around... "What about all the white kids I hear running around nowadays?"

"As for the Boulevards, they're not worth talking about. They're pussies. We had a couple scraps, then negotiated a peace."

"Heh. And *you* set the terms?"

"You know it. All we wanted was to go over to they malls. They can't keep us out, that's racist shit. We don't raise much trouble, just a little. But they had agreement with the Lubbs. Fuck that. Yost tunnel's open now, no civilians get harassed, black and white can cross both ways, no tagging in the tunnels, no selling shit down there. It's in the interest of the white humans too. Some of them like to come over and have adventures. No harm in it. Lubbs don't like it, but fuck them. They don't want white power flowing into the corner and disrupting they control, but they have to put up with being squeezed. Jack-Rabbit Lubbs get no love from other Family clicks; there's warring time-to-time across the ocean. Besides, they can profit a little too from the whites bring money to they hoes. Consequence, we also get money from whites bringing money in our dice games. And we can shop for white ass from the girls in they mall."

"Goddamn, man. Sounds like you got everything in hand. Everything."

"Eventually the Jack-Rabbit Lubbs are going to be finished—all the drugs and all the hoeing—and there'll be a clean neighborhood from here to the tracks. That can be S·M·F land, or it can just come out from under gang control. The Boulevards can be dominated anytime. But first we gotta organize."

"S·M·F?"

"Come on. Serious Mother Fuckers. Sammy just said that."

5.

WHEN EFREM GOT OUT OF JUVIE, I brought him in, and he taught us a little about stealing cars. That would eventually be a big money maker, but for the time being we contented ourselves with gambling money and loans. I brought Kenneth Branch in too, and he was real helpful in that department. Kevin Carter was instrumental because he'd made his reputation by setting up a sports book in school—he was still a student. It was tough for him at first to carve out a business because he had to muscle out some white kids who wanted a sports-book monopoly. One of them was nephew of a Master-Race gangster. But when the Nazi motherfucker got locked up, Kevin took over the market, focusing on black students first, then extending to the Latins. Some of the whites preferred him too, but he let them go where they wanted after brokering a deal with the white bookies. Sometimes compromise is best.

Jonas kept me close, and I got officially appointed to the position of *teachor*. My moniker was Brain. My responsibilities included rule-drafting—in consultation with Jonas and the O.G.s; writing the S·M·F lit; brainstorming new hustles; teaching babies; discerning candidates for recruitment; and being reasonable in the face of bullshit.

One of my first brainstorms was creating a pair of numbers games for Kevin to introduce alongside his sports-book. I was the original creator of *All-or-Nothin'* and *Give-me-Somethin'*. On an *All-or-Nothin'* ticket you could pick five numbers from one to ten. On a *Give-me-Somethin'* ticket you picked two numbers. On Fridays we shuffled up ten cards, ace-to-ten, and drew five at random, with witnesses. For *All-or-Nothin'*, if we hit all your numbers, or none of them, we paid 110-to-1. For *Give-me-Somethin'*, if we hit both your numbers, we paid 3-to-1. We got a lot of action on these games, we made a lot of money, and the sports-book business went up when we offered some discounts on numbers tickets to winners of sports bets. We were always honest with these games.

One other task was to draw up a list of the S·M·F seed members, the O.G.s and soldiers that started it all, and produce a mini-biography for our early history. Here's the result of that:

<u>O.G.s (NAME—*Moniker.* Bio.)</u>

JONAS DANDRIDGE—*Cloud.* Heart and soul a gangster dedicated to the betterment of his S·M·F brothers and the larger community. Lifetime appointment to the post of *Generol.*

THAYNE SEALS—*Proven.* Courage and Loyalty, risen from hardship, incapable of fear or regret. Strong. First appointee to the position of *Muckamuck.*

KEVIN CARTER—*President.* Playful but strong, a natural organizer with an eye for business opportunity, and possessor of mad respect. No official appointment, but recognized as de facto gamblemastor.

MALAPHA JUDSON—*Brain.* First veteran and recognized assaultor. Brain-skill possessor. First appointed *Teachor.*

RICK PETTIS—*Coca-Cola.* In with the crew from before there was a crew. Doesn't need anyone, but loves his brothers nonetheless. Appointed *Quartermastor.* Once complained at a McDonalds that the cola didn't have enough syrup and got saddled with an unfortunate nickname. Learned to live with it.

PHILIP COLEMAN—*Lettuce.* Known forever. Smiles too much. Appointed *Money-Man.*

Captains (NAME—*Moniker*. Bio.)
(This Post is Temporary, Subject to Reassignment)

DUANE ARTERBERRY—*Solid*. A physical presence like none other, but his body's not as big as his soul.

KENNETH BRANCH—*Fierce*. Quality card-playor, mentor to the young, and angle-shootor supreme.

JEFF STEWARD—*Horseback*. The guy kids look at when they want to know "what's next?"

EFREM BOSTIC—*F*. Generator of much cash thanks to his contacts and mechanical know-how. Very careful and calculating in his thievery, but in other aspects his motto is "Leap always, look never."

Soldiers (NAME—*Moniker*. Bio.)

SAMMY BENJAMIN—*Temple*. Not an O.G., not a Captain, not Jewish, but somehow more influential than most of us thanks to his official appointment to the post of *Jestor*. Envied by all and annoying as fuck.

DAVE SIMMONS—*One-Time*. Wants everyone to know about his total disregard for danger. We had to rein him in or he'd self-destruct. Kind of borderline dependable, but surely better than any sucker outside the click.

DARAN JACKSON—*Flower*. Hung up a little too much on women to be an O.G., though he was there from the beginning.

Kevin Jenkins—*Keychain.* A converted wild-child. Lives by the rules always. We provide him with the guidance society failed to provide. Constantly practices his card skills.

Ivan Adell—*Terrible.* Life-lover in all circumstances, but he can put on a serious face like nobody. You gotta live with this guy for months before you realize how damned funny he is.

John Williams—*Toothless.* Don't let him drive.

Delton Robinson—*Ace.* Very physically skillful and precise. Plays pool like a pro. Can knock out a kid twice his size, which is good since he's not that big.

Isaac Damond—*Young.* Faced death twice and survived, including a childhood head injury (hammer blow) and taking a bullet in the lung from a Black Steel Nines assault. Bounces back every time.

John Thomas—*Too-Tall.* His name is not ironic. Neither is his nickname. Has no bad habits that are unapproved.

Mark Simms—*Market.* Sold some guns before he hooked up with us, which was a habit he had to break. We let him play with knives a lot so he can sublimate.

Richard Echols—*Rollup.* Presumably he can fight, though he may never have to prove it because he's so damn ugly humans run on sight.

Walter Jones—*Jelly.* When he sees tits, he goes fucking crazy. Someday we might have to blind him.

MICHAEL WILLIAMS—*Bank*. Gets a lot of lending business, and no one yet has missed a payment. Might be charmed this way. Denied his own father a loan, and we still laugh about that.

BLAISE GRANT—*Amazin'*. This guy has a story worth telling on its own, but it would take a whole book. It's too complicated to get into right now. Reads German, which is just insane.

JAMES HARRIS—*Thunder*. A real morale driver who can hype us up to double our strength and courage. Can also shame anyone if he calls you out. Sleeps like eleven hours a day, though, and no one wants to wake him up.

MARCIO CLEMMONS—*Hardcore*. Killed his sister and was reported on TV. Surprisingly cool despite. Keeps his shit together by unanimous O.G. consent.

DANIEL MAGAZINE—*Clip*. Ever-present. Seriously, if I ever forget to mention he's with us at some point, he's there. He always tries to resolve arguments by telling us what he remembers... and no one even knows when he's watching. Spooky, actually.

PATRICK JACKSON—*Smooth*. A total liar who gets violated repeatedly. His transgressions are always minor, but stupid. Somehow we keep him around.

CRAIG TOUSSAINT—*Nap*. Really very seriously black. Can pull the top off a beer bottle with his eye. Doesn't talk much, though.

GLENN ROBINSON—*Hops*. Diceor. Has a Puerto Rican girlfriend and never brings her around to meet the boys. Had decent parents and probably had the best chance of living a normal life, but he chose us anyway, he's loyal, and he can fight.

WOODROW DANTZLER—*Dancer.* Good at basketball. Good-hearted and almost stupidly optimistic, like a puppy dog waiting at the door of an owner who went away to Florida and forgot him. We don't understand him, but he cheers us up.

CURTIS JONES—*Rootwork.* We're a little creeped out by Curtis at times, but we know he got powers. It's a good thing we're not allowed to get stoned, or he'd probably put us all under a spell. No one wants to taste his gumbo.

✤

Others joined later, but surprisingly few. We stayed tight-knit, and Jonas did an excellent job in recruiting the best from the start, with Sammy and Thayne helping him weed out the less-than-best. Many hangers-on stayed babies for life, never suited to soldier status.

There were a few official posts as detailed above. Only *Generol* was a lifetime appointment. The others could be re-assigned, and it was assumed the number of captains could increase as the gang grew, as an incentive for soldiers to distinguish theyselves.

Kevin "Keychain" Jenkins, Ivan "Terrible" Adell, and Glenn "Hops" Robinson were our most prized gamblors, so Kevin Carter organized them and put them under Kenneth Branch's captainship for direct oversight. This is where team specialization began.

6.

OUR CLICK PLAYED SEE-LOW. We played a lot among ourselves, and sometimes there was a lot of money in it, but usually just whatever we had, not much. But there was a strict honor code, we wouldn't cheat. It didn't happen. You didn't have to be careful or watch out to see that no one was cheating, because we had our honor. Except, of course, for the metarule. If you were a *sucker*, we could cheat you. I mean, if you were not in the S·M·F, there's no point in thinking we were going to play fair. Not that we advertised it. Even when Flower wanted to introduce his cousin, he asked around in advance, "let's play fair with this guy"—no. If anyone wasn't S·M·F, we could take his money. Baby gangsters or affiliates, maybe we'd cut some slack. Outside suckers, no. Not that the money was a lot, it wasn't. We weren't high-rollers back then. And for you who's curious, if you don't know how cheating works, forget it, it's not like we could win all the time. It's not like the movies.

One Afro, Hops, he was our See-Low expert. He could stop a six on one die about one-third of the time—as opposed to the one-sixth you get fairly. That's one die, you can't put a stop on two dice or three, there's no method for that. We didn't play loaded dice, there's no loaded dice or shaving, but he was the mechanic, he could stop a six pretty good. That might not sound like much, but listen. The difference is, no cheating, you get about two-and-a-half percent when banking, and you lose two-and-a-half when fading. A lot of suckers don't even know that, they don't see the bank gets an edge, so if you don't even know that, you were losing when we encouraged you to fade all the time. But trying to stop a six, with Hops's success rate, he got like eight percent as bank—that's huge!—and he even got an edge of just over half a percent when fading. If you want to know the real numbers, it was like 8.17% banking, and 0.61333% fading. If he was fading as much as he was banking—and that's pretty much true with him because we liked him to get most of the action and we promoted him as an action player—then he was getting nearly as much as an American roulette wheel gets for the house.

Ivan, he was like Hops's apprentice, he learned fast and he could stop a six with about one-quarter accuracy. That got him a little over five percent banking, but he was still losing about one percent fading. He claimed to break even when fading, but it's not true. He was lucky a bit, and he didn't understand variance. Overall, that got him something closer to a European roulette wheel, not quite as good as an American wheel, but it was okay.

By the way, these guys didn't know the numbers, I had to calculate all that shit myself, and I observed when they practiced, and I tried to figure an estimate on how good they were on stopping. What they knew was the technique, and they knew they were winning.

Now, sometimes you gotta throw fair for a while, because some suckers try to get wise, and sometimes when the bank's got a low point you stop a four or a five because too many sixes might look suspicious. In some cases we pulled some silly shenanigans, like when one of our guys was fading against another S·M·F, and at the same time a sucker was fading, our guy would jump up and obstruct his view of the dice for a second... not that we knew what the dice were going to show, but it gave a second to fix the fall if it was a 1-2-3 or something. Our guy sometimes got angry on the sucker's behalf, too, which you'll see is something works really well in three-card monte when I get to talking about that.

But See-Low... it's not like Hops and Ivan could roll thousands of times a night, and suckers didn't come around with a lot of money anyway, so there was not much in it overall. And it wasn't a fix, sometimes suckers walked away with money, sometimes they didn't, but as far as they could tell it was fair, no one was robbing them, etcetera. So most nights, we could maybe afford to buy a few extra bottles of Midnight Dragon for the click from what we earned, with Hops and Ivan supplying most of the profit. We used to buy Midnight Dragon a lot in the 64-ounce bottles just because it was cheap, and it's more massive than a forty, but seriously, after a while I was too old to drink that shit anymore. It was fun when we were kids.

Three-card-monte's another story! That game we were playing outside our count, we were playing white humans, all kinds of humans, and humans we would never see again. In that game it was pure murder, no one got a dollar out of us. It still amazes me how green most suckers are. I mean, who don't know three-card-monte is an unbeatable fix? Do you want to know how to tell who's a shill in the game? If you ever see a guy pick up even one extra dollar than he put on the table, even one time, that guy's a shill, guaranteed. And yet the suckers fall for it all the time. Even the smart ones. Especially the smart ones. They so smug they think they got you figured out. Or they believe that common bullshit that the dealer lets you win occasionally just to get you hooked. No. You already hooked, and dealers don't give away dollars. But these suckers will empty they wallets and give up they gold watches sometimes, thinking they got you figured. It couldn't really get me to shed any sympathetic tears because they were so damn dumb!

We liked to operate the busses because it provided a lot of extra opportunity. The basic plan was, sticks and shills got on about a stop or two before the mechanic. The blend happened, you know. Sometimes it was two sticks and one shill, and we reserved a shill to get on four stops later. The operator got on—and I tell you, how many suckers think a three-card-monte dealer operates alone? Incredible! So it looked like this guy got on the bus, and on a whim he started promoting a game, a few players got in, oh what fun! The shills sometimes won a bit, the suckers got involved, the sticks stirred up interest. The suckers of course couldn't catch a break, but they saw at least some guys were winning, right? And that was pretty much it most of the time, dealer got off when no one was too interested anymore, or they'd given up, rest of the team got off separately wherever they were planning to go. But when trouble happened, the sticks could always fix it. There were rare occasions when a real hot sucker tried to start a fight, where a stick took on the role of bigger aggressor. He shouted bloody murder at the dealer and the dealer knocked *him* out! At that point, with the distraction and all, and the sucker seeing someone just got beat down... he was kind of beat by proxy, right? And by that time the dealer was already off the bus.

That's rare, we didn't take it to that level almost never, but smaller shenanigans like just a small fuss would usually do. Sometimes the sticks even dragged the dealer off the bus like they were going to fuck him up, and meanwhile they'd all got off with all the money. And Ivan—he lived up to his name, man, he was so damn terrible—he looked older than his age, so he liked to play like he was an undercover cop sometimes to break up a game when the dealer needed an excuse to exit. One time though, I can't believe it, Ivan got up to bust up a game with his cop routine, and meanwhile an *actual* undercover cop got up at the same time. The pig was going to make a grab for the dealer, and Ivan stepped in and was like "Excuse me, you're going to have to show me some I.D.," and meanwhile the dealer and one stick broke for the door as the bus had just stopped. The cop tried to push past, but Ivan persisted, and the cop showed I.D., then demanded Ivan's. Ivan said, "I lost it."

Oh, my God! That drives me crazy just thinking about it. Fucking balls, man. Of course Ivan had to do two months, but worse could have happened. Jail time's no fun, but when you go through that baptism of fire and you come out stronger, that adds to the strength of the crew.

We were a real small click without many connections. That's why we were iron, though, on an individual level.

Now, one more thing on the three-card-monte games, though, I should tell you. We almost never had to rob anyone, but it happened sometimes. Sometimes suckers made it happen. You just shouldn't fuck with a game when it's in operation, and when you did, we either had to have a clear exit, or it was you and us, and "us" was five guys. If you put us to that cost of effort, we got reimbursed.

7.

THERE WAS this kid named "Kid" who wasn't the type to associate with our click, but he was friends with one of our associates named Damitri. But Damitri isn't important to this story except for how he brought Kid into the picture. Damitri was cool enough, but not really soldier material, and Kid even less so.

When I was introduced to Kid, I didn't even want to talk to him, and I definitely didn't want to let any other O.G. or captain meet him. With my influence in gangster discernment, if I said "No" to someone, they had no chance of getting brought into the click, and they'd be a fool even to try to associate. But Damitri kept bringing Kid up in conversation and talking to Horseback and F about him. Efrem said "Fuck no," but Horseback—who was Damitri's only ally with any pull—thought we could get some advantage from using Kid's house as a kind of party spot in the Corner. He had a grudge against the Lubbs and he wanted to get under they skins a little.

Against my will, one time when we were hanging at "the beach," I got pulled into a conversation. Jonas was present.

"Why the fuck I'm even hearing his name again?" I asked. "He's no good, and he never going to be any good."

"He's not that bad," said Horseback.

"Not bad is not good. If he's not iron, I don't want to hear about it. Talk about a fucking ant if you want."

"It's not even about that. We can just exploit him, or whatever; we don't have to be his friend."

"What exploit? What's he got we even want?"

"We don't rob," said Jonas. He threw that idea right off the pier. "We better than that."

"So what? We don't have to rob him, and we don't have to make him S·M·F, but I'm just saying six or eight guys could hang out. He got a nice location."

"Nice shithole for the Corner. Your even acting like a friend to him is doing him a big favor. He has no charisma. We could hang out at Buggle's Brew if we want a new spot."

"No we can't. They don't even let us in there, even with a fake I.D."

Efrem jumped in now.

"What's in it? What you want to do? Rape his mom while he watches?"

"Maybe. I'm just bored. I want to stir up some shit."

Jonas came in with a proposal to turn the conversation around.

"You want to get in some trouble, I got an assignment for you. You take Market, Dancer, and Bank. Dancer's the only one with break-in experience among you, so you learn from him. No strong-arming. You get out of the city and get up to Kensal or Quinwood for a few days. Find a nice little house with likely jewelry. You get in they house when they out, and you bring me that shit, and if there's a car in the garage, you bring that too. If you find hooks, long-guns, that's cool, we can sell that shit, but don't bring me any electronics."

"Four niggers in Kensal?"

"The fuck you say?"

"Afros, I mean. And white humans have alarms."

"Why do you think that is?"

There was a little silence while we pondered.

"Why me, anyway? Blaise's already got a fine burglary crew put together, and they don't go fucking around in white villages."

"We gotta diversify, and it's time to take your learning to the higher level. Then you can stop talking about making trouble where we don't need it because you're bored. There's no time in life for boredom."

Horseback really smiled, and I could tell he was hyped for this mission despite his protests.

And... mission accomplished.

Meanwhile we were still making paper from gambling, which we always did because it was fun and easy. I added a kind of primitive Chuck-a-Luck variant to our repertoire based on a game I saw some Korean-Constellation gangsters running downtown. In our version, you just tossed three dice and bet a number, one to six, and if any dice hit your number we paid even money. This was a game for the dumbest of suckers who couldn't see we had the edge, thinking three dice out of six is half, right? But we didn't even offer any bonus odds for hitting a pair or three-of-a-kind like a traditional Chuck-a-luck, because I thought that was like tacitly saying you should expect us to give odds. We got fifteen and three-quarters percent without even having to cheat, so we let the suckers throw the dice theyselves. At first I thought we should make the player throw dice from a cup, but then I realized no skills were good enough to beat our odds, and skilled players wouldn't be fool enough to play anyway, so hand-tossing was allowed.

But gambling, for all the fun, was small potatoes, and soon our main business came from car-thieving and loaning, with an occasional burglary-raid for thrills.

When our capital got big enough, loaning turned a lot of profit, and we could sometimes parlay. For instance, gang rules wouldn't let us *jack* cars, we could only steal them when the owner was out of sight, and we couldn't wield weapons. Some of us remembered how hard it was to ride a bike in our neighborhood because we'd get them jacked by Nines or unaffiliated hoodlums, and Jonas wasn't going to encourage us in that kind of thuggish behavior. But at the same time, it was legit for us to use violence, on rare occasions, in the performance of debt collection, and often our debtors, out of fear, turned to various crimes to raise the money they needed to pay us off. We didn't sell drugs, but maybe our debtors did. We didn't jack. They might. None of us S·M·F would be directly implicated. And one time a big debt led to a big heist.

An Afro named Paul, who had been discharged from the army years back and was now in security, got deep in our debt, and he was a gambling addict. It was clear he wasn't going to get together the money to pay us. We didn't normally back a guy with such a high chance of default, but Paul was chief of parking security for the mall over in Whiteville—Boulevards territory. So, under pressure, Paul agreed to send one mall-cop home early on a Saturday evening and take over his post, when lots of humans were in watching the latest new-release movies and gobbling up Bennigan's steaks. Then Paul watched while Efrem and his team drove off with seven cars from the lot. Efrem and Flower had the nuts to go back for a second round, so that made it nine. Meanwhile Paul took the cash from the booth collected from parking fees, he paid off half his debt, and we forgave the rest and bought him a ticket out of town.

He probably should have run from us early rather than play along with our schemes, but he must have been afraid of getting hunted. Besides which, he seemed to think until the last minute he could gamble his way out of debt, but he only got deeper in it.

Three BMWs, a Benz, an Audi, two 'Vettes, an IROC, and a Mazda. There was a Porsche on the lot, but it was too secure and too visible to run with, and a Jaguar, but no one knew how to steal one of those.

When we got nice cars, we sometimes cruised our neighborhoods for a while. It was cool to see the younger kids looking up to us, and some men too, working low-wage jobs and thinking *Damn, I'll never get a car like that.* And to think we used to walk around scared in our own neighborhood. Our own damn home, and we had to be scared of some shit happening, but now we were never scared. Looking around, we saw most humans most of the time were scared. Sometimes scared of us, and sometimes admiring. Some of us thrived on the fear we inspired because it made us fearless. But I know Jonas thrived on the admiration.

We didn't keep cars long at all though. Usually we got them into garages within a few hours. Efrem was getting mad influential because he'd developed some powerful contacts, including Association gangsters who bought cars off us at a good price. I don't know how he swung it, really. He had networking skills to go with his thieving skills, plus he wasn't too prejudiced against the whites when they could do business to our mutual advantage.

❧

Then Horseback got shot coming out of Kid's house, despite our warning not to let Kid associate. Horseback had been alone at the time, but questions revealed he had sometimes brought S·M·F wannabes in the Corner with him to put a thumb in the eye of the Lubbs.

Six of us went to see Horseback in the hospital to find out the details. Thayne was one of us, and Sammy was there. And a new guy, Troy Jackson, nicknamed Heaven, who'd been a soldier for a few months. Rootwork and Dancer too.

"I got missed by the first shot," Horseback explained. "Then I dodged and got hit by the second blast through a parked car."

Horseback got glass and buckshot in the face, neck, and upper chest, but survived it.

"If dude used a sabot, you'd been dead," said Dancer.

"Nah," said Thayne. "If he used a sabot, you wouldn't have been hit. Lubbs shoot sloppier than they clean they houses."

"What were you doing, Jeff?" I asked.

Horseback tensed up, then slumped.

"Look, it's nobody's business but mine, but I've been fucking Kid's girl-cousin lives in the Corner."

"Ha! What I say?" boasted Sammy.

"She just asked me to look in on him sometimes, so I stopped by for a few beers with his kin. They nice."

"And you stirred up the shit just like you wanted to, right?"

Sammy pounded Horseback on top of the head once to make him wince.

"You could say that."

"I'm going to knock them pellets out your face so you don't need surgery, eh?"

Despite his constant plays at humor and the challenges he seemed to pose for authority, Sammy's position as Jestor also required him to be a strict enforcer of gang discipline.

"Kid and his mom's just been getting harassed by Family of Man, is all."

"But," I said, "we don't do charity for some punk who can't defend hisself. Fams never wanted him, so he's surely not good enough for us."

Then Thayne spoke up with our verdict.

"O.G.s already talked about this. You're losing your captaincy, and your violation's going to be damn strict. But you're still a soldier."

"Thanks. Thanks, Thayne. Mala."

After we came back from the hospital, Jonas dispatched a group of eleven of us, headed by me and President, to go visit Kid and see what was his story. We were walking together in a tight pack through the corner, joking among ourselves and making our presence known and felt in what was supposedly

Family-of-Man territory—because we never had any regard for the fucking Lubbs—and now that Horseback was shot, it was time to show strength. We were unarmed, except for knives, per our usual taboo, but we were going to jump on anybody who looked at us funny—little children and old ladies excepted.

Then out popped two shooters from a doorway and blasted. One with a shottie, one with a hook. We scattered by instinct—there was like an electric current in the air so we were charged and moving without reason—but Carter kept cool and he had three guys close-grouped behind him—and then they just spontaneously surged forward, fuck all. I raced to join them, and together we laughed to see the shooters break north. Not a one of us was hit, and I'd counted two shotgun blasts and five-or-so pistol cracks. All together we had such an unvincible feeling it cannot be described. Nap was the only one who'd had some stuffing torn out his coat by a bullet-graze, and not a mark on his flesh, and I think he was the proudest of us all for that miracle moment.

There was one more *fuck-you* blast from the shotgun—about a block and a half away now—and that was all.

I don't think we even stopped to consider regrouping or returning to our count. I was the Brain, but no one consulted me. Only one guy, I forget who, stopped to make a phone call on the way, to let Jonas know what was up. Then we arrived outside Kid's place. And the block was quiet. Dark for the most part.

Kid refused to open the door, so we forced it.

"Don't call the cops. We just want to talk to you!"

We got in the hall, but Kid had locked hisself in the bathroom before we got to him. So we let him chill in there while we looked around and then relaxed in the living room. His mom and uncle was out. It was just us and him. We watched the game on his TV, and drank what we could find in the fridge.

We talked, of course, but I was not of the opinion Kid

had much to do with anything. He wasn't a gangster. On the other hand, a lot of guys thought it suspicious the Lubbs shot only Horseback, not Kid. Plus he didn't open the door when we asked nicely.

In twenty minutes, Jonas and Thayne arrived, plus Solid and Jelly. They'd parked two blocks away, then hoofed it. Jelly had a bag.

"Alright, what's up?" Thayne asked.

But Jonas just said, "Bring him out."

We got the bathroom door open by kicking it. At first we just made some noise, but Solid put some force in, and with two or three kicks with the flat of his foot, the jamb splintered. There was some ruckus getting all of us in through that narrow doorway. Kid was crouched in the shower stall by that time, with no exit, and he had no weapon, so there was nothing he could do. We got fingers in his hair and twisted up his hands and shit, and he made a kind of girlish cry when Coca-Cola twisted his neck and head, but then, though he put up a fierce struggle of sorts, we pretty much got him immobilized in all his limbs... it was kind of like a cell extraction. I didn't like to think about it like that, but that's what it turned into. And then we got the fucker out through the house, bumping and shoving, and out on the stoop we threw him face-first down three brick steps. Before he could think of getting up, Dandridge had thrown a cinder-block down on the back of his head, hard. The block had been a smoking-stool sitting beside the door.

"Oh!"

"Damn, man, fucking sick!"

"Kid's rolling, man, like a animal."

Some of us had already got down the stairs and surrounded him just in case he had a way to make an exit. And though he was too fucked up to run or fight any more, we picked him up and knocked him around a bit, and then it was too late; I knew we were going to kill him. He was crying now, but you couldn't see the tears because his face was all washed and running from the blood.

"Get me a blade, man."

When Thayne said this, Kid heard it.

"No, no..." Kinda feeble.

Suddenly half the gang turned into errand boys, fetching tools to finish this motherfucker. Thayne got handed a knife and slashed at the kid's neck... had some fight in him yet, boy, but not enough... the blade jabbed him in the back and ribs a few times, then he got rolled over on his side on the pavement, and one more stab in the neck made it official. With the flailing around and kicking feet, Thayne still got in another stab, this time in the chest, then yanked out the blade and we all grabbed Kid, picked him up, flipped him face-down, and watched the blood flow out on the pavement, really pouring out.

His jittering stopped and he got limp, so we dropped him.

"Get me the hatchet, dude; get this fucker's fingers off." This was Thayne speaking again. Dandridge was still standing on the stoop, watching.

One-Time came forward with a hatchet—and Jelly stood there with his now-empty tool bag—and Thayne chop-chop-chopped so the fingers flew off one hand... and then the other.

"Trophies man. Get them. But don't finger your girlfriends with them." He cracked a smile. "We're serious motherfuckers, dude."

As for me, I got a thumb.

8.

AFTER THAT, the lid was off for two nights straight... I mean we were crazy... drinking all night and hollering... Cloud bought us three girls off Los Asesinos... I partied, drank a bit, smiled and laughed... tried to have fun and show it... to tell the truth, I didn't feel great about what we'd done. When I looked around, I noticed a few other guys—Keychain, Ace, and Thunder—they looked like they were partying for show. It was an act for some of us. Jelly, though, was right in it, celebrating with the rest. But it never went spoken how we felt about it, except by Sammy, who made a mockery of our guilt by giving it an overblown and ridiculous expression.

"Oh my God, we're murderers. Murderers! Will I ever stop having nightmares about the blood? Ha ha. At what price do we buy our reputations for ruthlessness?"

"Shut up, Sammy!" said Jonas. "I'm telling you. We here to have fun tonight. Breathe easy."

"I would breathe easy if you handed me that blunt."

"What blunt? This is a tobacco cigar, Sammy, we don't defile our bodies here."

"Tell that to the bitches in the back room," Coca-Cola interpolated.

But Sammy just pointed his finger at Jonas where he was sitting on the sofa beside Luis Gandara, a stranger to our group.

"You bloodstained puritan, don't you know?"

"What?"

"Reefer's not drugs, man. Reefer's a vegetable."

Later that night, Jonas invited me to join him and Gandara, Thayne and Lettuce for a little conference, and I got to know Gandara a little better (but not much). He was 22 and jaded.

"What you do for fun, Luis?" I asked him.

"This. Chill, you know. And sometimes picnic with the girls."

"Picnic?"

"Yeah, man. Heh. How you think I get my handsome tan? Gotta get my sun, you know, I'm the outdoors type when I get the chance."

"Can't much like this weather, then."

"Fuck this weather. No. I don't like it."

Lettuce took up another topic. "Hey, did you see that new Questing Beast movie? That was mad."

"No. What is that? Dragons and shit flying around. No, I didn't see it."

"Come on. That was nice! You don't have to be so serious. It gives you a kind of vision of what... you know, it's like to possibilities of the mind? I don't know how to explain it."

"Dragons are faggots, man, I don't like that kind of movie."

"Shit."

"That's not real."

"So... So, what is it? You want to watch a movie about guys who smoke cigars for five minutes and then scratch they balls? I tell you, you make a movie about what's real?—half the audience goes home that night and hang theyself, and that's the truth."

"I hear you."

Small talk didn't carry us very far, and Gandara wasn't talking business—at least not with me, and I didn't know what kind of business was going on anyway. But he seemed to bond well with Jonas for some reason. They talked seriously, but impersonally, about what they thought about the direction society was taking. But I faded in and out of the conversation so I couldn't report what it was all about.

At the end of the night, Gandara walked out with a $50,000 cash loan, interest free, which he paid back promptly at the end of the week, per arrangement. Jonas explained he used the money to arm up some gangsters with long-guns to take care of business with some La Fuerza Latina rivals in a neighboring count. We swung them several more interest-free loans through the years in exchange for sending us girls to break in for they hoeing business, and for security in case any S·M·F wound up in adult prison. Los Asesinos had a lot of pull inside.

9.

Rules for Females

RULES of Women and Girls:

- No female will ever be an S·M·F, and they are not to be encouraged to hang around as wannabe affiliates.

- If we are to do any business with females, they must be affiliated with they own separate gang, and any alliance will be temporary and provisional.

- If an S·M·F has sex with a girl, and if she's not a ho, then she is now *claimed*, and thus permanently off-limits to any other S·M·F or affiliate. It don't matter if the S·M·F wants to cut her loose, or he cheats on her, or he gets with other women, she cannot be "unclaimed". Even if she turns ho outside the gang, she is not released from claimed status with regards to the gang.

- If a girl has been paid for sex before being claimed, she a ho. If an O.G. buys a girl for the house, or if he invites an unclaimed girl and declares her "for the house," then she becomes a ho. A ho cannot ever be claimed; they are free agents. Don't be jealous over hoes.

- A sister of an S·M·F is not a ho and cannot be claimed. She's kin to all of us, and thus off-limits. If you wouldn't fuck your sister, don't fuck mine. And if you would? Get ready to be *killed*.

- Half-sisters are sisters.

- First cousins are not sisters, but they remain off-limits except by special arrangement by permission of the direct relative and approval by O.G.-council resolution.

- No female of any sort may sleep for more than three consecutive nights or five days in a month in the clubhouse or on S·M·F property.

- Attention teen runaways: Find you a partner to claim you, or keep running. We don't have long-term "just friends" relationships. Requests to be declared "for the house," to secure a home and free-agency or to otherwise freeload, will be rejected out of hand.

- Note: blowjobs and anal count as sex, so be careful. It's easier to claim a girl than you think.

10.

A LITTLE WHILE AFTER our party-mania faded, when things were getting back to the normal grind, someone drove up and shot into Jonas's house, which had become our general headquarters and clubhouse (the downstairs neighbors moved out the basement and Jonas bought it so he could have the whole house). There was several of us there at the time, but only Cookie got hurt: a bullet through the knee that had come through the wall. (Cookie was a recently recruited soldier who didn't have any fighting skills, any reputation, or any exceptional strength of character, but he could cook some excellent food we all appreciated. He could be called the one exception to our usual recruitment standards.)

We took it as a fair guess it was the Jack-Rabbit Fams trying to sweat us. We didn't talk to the police about it, and we played dumb when they came around to ask questions.

None of the questions were about Kid; he wasn't a part of the conversation. We figured, with the Jack-Rabbit Fams also warring with the Grogan Fams across the ocean, 5-0 was otherwise occupied.

"The cops have to know the truth of what happened, though," said Lettuce.

"What the cops know or don't know, I don't know," said Sammy. "But no one's making a fuss over Kid."

"Typical," Jonas moaned. "Cops just don't give a fuck about a black kid's death."

"Not with his mom and uncle disappearing like I heard," said Cola.

"Well, look at you, bitch!" said Sammy to Jonas. "You seriously going to whine about police apathy when you're the one to benefit?"

"It's not like I want to go to jail, but shit."

"Screw down," said Thayne.

"Lid off," said Sammy.

❧

After that, there was a shooting in Brandywine park. Co-ca-Cola caught it in the belly and the neck. I was there beside him. When he lay curled up on the ground, he said, "there's still time." He said it twice. But I don't think he knew what he was saying; I don't think he even understood an ambulance was coming for him; I don't know what he wanted time for. By the time the ambulance arrived, he'd been unconscious for five minutes, and he never recovered.

The whole click was torn up about it. It was a disaster. I never saw so many tears as I saw in the next three days, and also at the funeral.

A white kid from across the tracks also died in the shooting. He was "an honors student," and a "good kid," who was reportedly "slumming it" with a black girlfriend, and hanging out in the park at the wrong time. Wrong time, wrong place. His death brought some media attention to our neighborhood, and there was a report on the theme of "Gangland Spreads its Influence."

I believe that kid *was* a good kid. But so was Rick Pettis. And nobody was saying it.

Hardcore Marcio got some airtime, though—right time, right place—and in his interview he brought some attention to the truth of our situation.

"We all about positivity here. No drugs, no guns. We have a clean community, kids just want to have fun, but we don't ask for this trouble."

The reporter said, "It's been said the 'Black Steel Nine' gang is trying to expand its territory, and drugs are being sold in Brandywine Park."

"There's no truth in that whatsoever. Whatever they do on they side of Silver Ave, we got no beef with the Nines as of now, that's been long squashed. We're a peaceful community, but we sick of what's going on. Family of Man is the start of our troubles, but it's really the drugs and the guns in general, because that's what this is. We strong enough to say 'No, we don't want that.' But the S·M·F, we get no support out here. We know the city just forgotten about us, and we out here risking our lives to make it safer."

"What is S·M·F? Can you explain?"

"Society's Moral Foundation, man. And Cloud is the savior of our neighborhood. We the ones going to make it right."

Following up on this brief moment of fame, Jonas called around to local journalists until he found a downtown magazine, *The Agitator*, that was willing to interview him on the positive effects the S·M·F could have on our community. He hyped up the idea our "organization" was born of necessity; society at large, politicians, schools, authorities, and our own families left us to fend for ourselves in a hostile environment, surrounded by thugs and pushers, so the only solution was to force a restructure of the social order on a local level: peers supporting peers, offering ethical guidance, enforcing an honor code, promoting self-reliance, and preventing the demoralization or enslavement of youthful minds.

For reasons unknown, the interview was never published.

Jonas also assigned me the task of writing grant-proposals to see if we could get any money from the state or federal government to support our movement. In between other tasks, I dedicated about seven months to this, but no money materialized. Not a dime. And at the same time, we gave five hundred dollars to a community gardening center was beautifying a couple of nearby vacant lots and taught children how to care for plants. One of the lots, unofficially, got known as "Morality Garden."

Other than that it was business as usual on the gambling, loaning, and thieving fronts, plus we had to take care of business with the F.O.M.

❧

Horseback broke his hands and took a serious beating when he assaulted Leeshawn Lavant at the F.O.M.'s favorite barber shop. Leeshawn was the chief of the Jack-Rabbit Lubbs, and he escaped without much harm, while Horseback, in the process of his beatdown by four or five guys, wrecked half the shop and got arrested for it. The Lubbs would probably have preferred to kill him, but there was too many civilian witnesses in the midafternoon.

Lubbs broke up two of our dice games by shooting into the crowd, and that drove away the suckers from coming in our area for a while, but the second time it happened we managed to catch one of them when the crew started to pull out. We fucked him up pretty good, but didn't kill him because his friends came back quick to drive us off.

Solid was the one tackled that kid from the side when his attention was distracted—it was a heroic move—but he wouldn't stop blaming hisself for letting the shooter go when his boys came back blasting.

"For all we know, he could be the one shot Cola."

"Nah, that other guy was taller, I'm telling you."

"Humans always look taller when they killing."

There were no deaths in these clashes, but one civilian lost an eye.

Some of us took to driving around the Jack-Rabbit Corner just to menace humans. Then it became a kind of game where new affiliates got sent in to see if they could get shot at. But the Lubbs were laying low around that time because they conflicts with the Grogan Lubbs were getting very hot, so I guess they didn't want to get embroiled in anything new.

Two of our guys we'd just hooked up with, "Knockdown" Lonnie Battle and "Maximum" Max Thomas, got initiated as soldiers after they pulled off a pretty cool stunt. They took a shitty old van they stole, stuffed it full of books, paper, and garbage, and crashed it outside the Fuck Club—The Lubbs' favorite whorehouse—and burned the van at one in the morning. Consequence, they drew fire from multiple shooters and escaped on foot after a long chase.

But we weren't getting any closer to avenging Coca-Cola's death, and the soldiers knew it wasn't right. Arguments went from "Why don't we attack civilians if we can't get to the F.O.M. captains," to "Fuck the rules, let's get guns," but Jonas wouldn't compromise. So then a bunch of us went out for Chinese.

11.

"ALRIGHT, we got—what—seven pepper steaks... whose is that? Fierce, you got a pepper steak?"

"Nah. Lo mein."

"Lo mein, sir?"

"That's right."

"Very good! Let's not forget to tip. And four more pork lo mein... you just put it down, we'll sort it out... I'm serious, no blame, just put it down... and one chong-ding-dong..."

"That's Kung Pao Chicken, fool, and it's mine."

"They got Ding Dongs here?"

"Nah, figure of speech."

"So what else, egg rolls... pork fried rice... should we get some more food—what—General Tso's Chicken to share, or maybe wings?"

"Why not both?"

"That's a lot of food."

"What's the budget on this?"

"No budget. Jonas is paying."

"Really. Well fuck it, get everything!"

"Yeah, exactly. I want General Tso's Chicken right next to my pepper steak, right next to my wings, and I'm not sharing a god damned thing."

"Especially not the check."

"Got that right."

"Excuse me, you want how many General Tso Chicken?"

"Call it eight."

"And how many wing?"

"Everybody. Thirteen."

"That will take long."

"Just bring them when you got them."

"Wait, what? Is Sammy going to eat *three* kinds of chicken? He's going to go into chicken shock."

"Nah, he got peanuts for vitamins."

"Who invited the scrubs? I thought captains and O.G.s only."

"Snot-and-Flower soup man, where it's at?"

"Y'all motherfuckers, man, can call me 'scrub' all you like, but soldiers be partying better than captains any day. Y'all turn everything into a meeting. 'What we going to do about this?' and 'I got a proposal for that.' Any time you can bend the O.G.s ears you think it makes you important. And y'all don't even have any girls in attendance, what the fuck is that?"

"If we bend the O.G.s ears, you break them with your nonstop gab. And didn't anyone ever tell you a *jestor* is supposed to be funny? You used to make me laugh man, now you just make me cry."

"Laughing is just another kind of crying."

"So if you don't like our company, why'd you come?"

"For the food, motherfucker, for the food."

"You know that Korean chick in the 'Look at my Legs and then Fuck Me' video?"

Flower was boasting to Jelly. Jelly just gave him a look.

"Claimed."

"No. No!"

"You know it."

"You can't just claim women off TV, you know. You gotta get with them."

"And?"

"No, I don't believe that shit. You claim every girl, and now you're picking them off TV? She not going to get with you. Why?"

"Why not?"

"She hot."

"Am I not hot? I'm a hot young buck with skills and power of persuasion."

"I need proof."

"Witness?"

He glanced at Sammy. Sammy put down his eggroll, wiped his lips, and replied in a blasé manner.

"It's true; it's a legitimate claim."

"Come on man. Not fair. You're not but nineteen years old, you're not rich..."

"So? I didn't ask her to marry me; I just asked her to fuck me."

"In so many words?"

"Basically."

"Oral?"

"Come on now. I took her at her word. 'Look at my legs and then fuck me.' Do you hear anything about oral in that sentence?"

"Damn."

"We met downtown. She was in the city to visit her cousin."

"The cousin looked better," said Sammy.

"And?"

"Claimed."

"Damn!"

"The cousin didn't look better, though, you just saying that. And anyway, she wasn't in no video."

"Wings, wings!"

"What, only three?"

"More coming."

"What you think about that kid I was telling you about? Hey. Hey, Mala! Brain. What you think about that kid Barry I was telling you about?"

"I don't remember. What were you telling me?"

"Come on, you know, Barry Love. I saw him knock out two guys, almost like magic. It was funny, man."

"No, don't listen, Mala. That kid is stupid, we heard that story, we don't need nothing to do with him."

"Shut up. What you know? It was funny, I'm telling you,

dude comes out—I don't know what the fuck started it—but dude dumps a half-eaten tub of popcorn on his head..."

"No, we already heard that story, come on. I want to hear... Jelly, tell about your last job."

"No, are you kidding me? I don't even want to tell it."

"Ha ha! I'm serious, this is funny, man."

"I don't ever want to do another garage heist in my life, I'm telling you."

"Tell it."

"Me and Nap were out. I was running the job, so I get in, get the ignition out... everything went smooth, it was like three and half, four minutes, no sign of anyone waking up, so I signaled Nap; he came out from his post down the block and pushed the car out..."

"What was it?"

"A Riviera. Anyway, Nap pushes us out, we get like... not far from the house... when I turn my head just to look and signal him... Fucking *dude is in the car!*"

"What?"

"Ha, ha, ha, ha. I told you man, it's fucking crazy!"

"How? Didn't you look around the car first?"

"I looked, I always look. I mean, I swear, but I don't know... I guess I didn't look."

"More wing here. Ten wing for everybody."

"Okay!"

"Sorry, could you please not shout. There are other customer."

"Come on. Who's spending as much money as us? Seriously. You want to tell us to quiet down?"

"I'm sorry, just please, okay?"

"Okay, okay."

"So what you do?"

"I fucking bugged. You know, the adrenaline shot up. I popped the door and ran out without even stepping on the brake."

"Ha, ha, ha."

"And?"

"And me and Nap did the right thing; we got the fuck out."

"What was the guy doing in the car?"

"Nothing, just lying on the back seat."

"That's not possible. Why?"

"You think I know?"

"But what happened to the car... your tools..."

"Tools are gone, man. The car rolled a bit down the hill... not much, just up on the curb and stopped."

"I don't buy it. What? The guy..."

"Maybe it was a mannequin or something."

"What's a guy going to be doing with a mannequin in his car? That's even a crazier story."

"I don't know, but what's a guy going to sleep in his own car in the garage, and he don't even wake up when the car is rolling down the hill and running up on the curb?"

"I don't even believe it. You probably saw a shirt and imagined the rest."

"I don't know, but I'm telling you, I'm not doing any garage jobs anymore."

"Cloud!"

"Yeah?"

"Jelly just volunteered. He wants five more garage jobs next month!"

"Ha!!!"

"That's right, Cloud, don't let him off the hook."

"Now, wait a fuck..."

"But you didn't have to run. You could have fought him or something."

Jonas piped up. "You been with us for how long," he said, "and you say that?"

"But..."

"He did right. You don't make more trouble, for what?"

"I know you're right. I'm just joking. But I'm thinking of

that white guy—what's his name—who beat a car owner to death with a slide-hammer."

"That's vicious," said Sammy.

"The circumstances were different. Sometimes you get put in a situation..."

"I know, Cloud, that's alright. But we could still sometimes use a hardcore guy like that. He got away too."

"He got away with the crime, but no car. Jelly got away with no car *and* no murder."

Sammy spoke up again. "You just prejudiced because the slide-hammer guy was white."

"Not true."

"Cloud, why don't you try, one more time, for the benefit of the new guy, to explain your policy on whites."

"What's to explain?"

Maximum kept his eyes on his food not to acknowledge he'd been made the object of conversation, though he was the only "new guy" present.

"Max," said Jonas, "You got a half-white half-brother, right? Well, I don't mean to disrespect your brother or stepmom or anyone else, but I'm just being practical. S·M·F needs unity."

"And unity is a strictly black phenomenon."

"Screw down, Sammy."

"Well, it's dark, anyway. Oh yeah, lid off."

"Look, you can tell me—and maybe it's true—some guy is hardboiled. Some white guys, they can be strong, and they can even be loyal to a black gang in normal circumstances. No problem. As long as you got them, and they got you, they might live for you and die for you and stand up for you when you need them. Great. But just let that white guy get arrested one time, and the whole shit falls apart. It's hard enough to find a black man that'll stand up for his brothers in that circumstance, believe me. But a white guy? No. They vulnerable."

"What do you think, Sammy?" asked Thayne. "Do you agree with what your generol is saying?"

"Huh?"

"He wasn't even listening."

"Heh."

"Always stirring up shit."

"Anyway, you getting educated, Max."

"I'm always eager to learn, man. I like the lifestyle."

"More soup. Where's the waiter? Where he been?"

"Yo, five more soups please!"

"You got it!"

"Why five?"

"It's a good number."

"What they make that shit out of, anyway? It tastes good, but it's kind of weird."

"I think you asked that question four times, and that's the kind of question you shouldn't ask once."

"You think they'll ever find out who sank that boat?"

"What boat?"

"Don't you follow the news?"

"No. Why? You my anchorman; you tell me, or I don't know."

"Come on, you don't know? The Cuban boat. Like eighty humans died. Some humans say the Coast Guard sank it, but Coast Guard say they weren't there. Maybe it was a torpedo. Maybe the Cubans got submarines now."

"What the fuck do I care about Cuban submarines?"

"Think about it man. Submarines."

"Heh, heh. You crazy. How'd this fucker get in our click. He should be locked up."

Dinner finished.

"Don't worry about anything nowadays," said Jonas after paying. "Things'll get handled. Captains, you take your teams out for they own celebrations. Keep up morale. And soldiers, stay strong."

We cheered, and moved out. And Sammy hooked his arm around mine and held tight.

"I'm sticking with you, Brain, until the real meeting happens. Nothing ever happens without you being there."

But as we moved towards the bus stop, Jonas didn't hang back, and the O.G.s intermingled with the others. Some of the crew split in various ways, while others mounted the bus. It looked like no "real meeting" was going to happen.

12.

THAT NEXT SATURDAY I had a date with this girl Shanda. It was our second date, and we went to a waterpark where she and her friends had permission from they parents to go without a supervisor—except there was one older girl kind of like a chaperone—she just didn't care what went on. Shanda's other friends also had boyfriends who arranged to meet them there.

Shanda was fifteen, so, old enough to know what she was doing.

The girls and guys mostly knew one another, and they were mostly upper-middle-class black kids, so I was kind of an alien there. But I didn't give much of a fuck what anyone else thought.

I got to say, though, Shanda was ravishing. I mean, a real knockout.

We had a good time, played around in the water, and roughhoused a bit. I wasn't much of a swimmer, but we enjoyed the slides, and I could get up close to her in her swimsuit and feel her smooth and sexy shoulders and back.

Our previous date, two weeks before, had gone well but chastely. We met at an Italian restaurant and ate upclass pizza pies. She had a curfew. The joint was pretty mainstream, but tolerable. And I'd been real honest with her. She knew something about my criminal past. Not much about my criminal present. For instance, I didn't tell her Efrem and I were out to rob some cars when I met her. But anyway, I'd approached her with confidence and swagger, and she knew me for a roughneck with an edge. And that didn't turn her off.

But now, at the top of a water slide, when we were sitting waiting our turn to go down, and I held her in my arms and wanted to move in for that first kiss, she looked up at me and said, "You're not going to hurt me are you?"

"Nah," I said, "I'm not going to hurt you." I got my kiss, and we went sliding down.

But that question really got its hooks in me. *Who is this girl?* I thought. And *Am I going to hurt her?*

At the bottom of the slide, after a few laughs and a few squeezes, I said to her, "You know, we should talk, actually."

And I got her alone for a while at a table in the snack bar.

"You know, what you said, that question—there's no reason I shouldn't ask you the same question. I mean, am I going to get hurt?"

"Really?"

"Yeah, I mean, you make things serious when you take that tone. It's not just fun and games when suddenly I have to worry about whether I *ever ever* might hurt you. Do I know the future beyond tomorrow?"

"Well, maybe I didn't have to mean it so seriously. But then, if you don't know beyond tomorrow, maybe if I did want to be serious..."

"I know you're younger, and I know I'm not the kind of guy you or your friends like to date, and maybe you think I'm tough because of how I carry myself with humans, you know, but don't assume I'm so insensitive I'm beyond caring."

"I didn't say that."

"I know."

"But... do you care?"

"That's a damn big question! You might be just the girl that could make me care though."

She looked bashful and... thrilled. And then a little less bashful.

"I shouldn't say anything, though," I said. "I mean, honestly... and I been honest with you... we need to know each other more intimately before we know enough to say how much we care."

"True."

"But don't assume you the only one taking a risk. You don't know how much I risk."

"You know just what to say. I'm going to trust you." She took my hand. "And next Thursday, my parents will be out, and if you know a place to take me, my sister won't say a thing if I disappear from the house for a few hours."

"Well, I can guarantee I'll arrange everything from there."

It happened. It was awkward having to tell the guys for the third time I couldn't hang out because of a girl, and it was *the same* girl and we hadn't had sex yet, so they knew she was a "nice" girl... I wasn't a virgin by any means. I'd been with hoes, and I'd even "claimed" a girl once—a white girl, and the sex was good with her the one time we did it, but otherwise there wasn't a connection, she was plain and nothing special and had no special care for me, just out for a thrill with a gangster one day. But Shanda really thrilled me in a way I can't describe. I took her to a motel. It was a dive, not because I couldn't pay for better, but because I felt a little less awkward and conspicuous there. I guess... I just knew the Indian guy at the motel wouldn't give a fuck, whereas a classy hotel would be asking for all kinds of I.D. and asking questions about her age and such. But we drank cognac and I picked her up in a four-year-old Cadillac I borrowed from Jonas—a legitimately purchased one, since the click had a few "keepers" we could drive risk-free. (I had a legitimate license as well).

And the sex was good in a way I didn't think it could be good. And it felt good just being with Shanda when we were talking and laughing and just looking at the walls. I felt like I was living a different life all of a sudden.

And she said to me, at the end of the night, though warm, and smiling, and full of tender charms, "It's really hard for me to say this. You were right that I have to take as much responsibility for this relationship as you. And I really hope to see you again, or hear from you. But I'll understand if I don't."

The S·M·F really didn't encourage serious relationships with girls, even though we had our rules in place just in case things went that way. I told details of my date to the other O.G.s and openly claimed her to the gang. It felt a little like a betrayal of Shanda to tell the blow-by-blow of our sex, but I didn't want to make the more serious betrayal of the gang that would come with silence. You got to be able to trust the boys with the details.

They sympathized. They said her attitude in the end was kind of fucked-up but expected. I didn't really see it that way, but didn't debate it. I had to figure things out for myself.

Jonas had Flower talk to me because he knew I was mixed up about Shanda. Flower and I were still old friends from the earliest days, but we didn't have much one-to-one chat-time anymore because of the class divide.

"Look," Flower said, "we got lives outside the S·M·F. I mean, we can be fully loyal, but there's things that are beyond the scope, and that's our own business. I mean some of these kids, they never going to get with anything but hoes, and some of the others are going to get too mixed up with girls turn they heads around too much and they don't know what they doing. They unsophisticated. But you got your rights to look for something better."

"I'm not girl-crazy or anything, I'm just thinking."

"Yeah, I know. And we different too, and that's cool. But I'm telling you, you know a lot, but women is something I know. I'm smoother than an S.P. pimp, I'm telling you."

"I've heard all your war stories."

"But what you need is the philosophy. Look, you're interested in something more, and I understand that."

"I don't know if I'm interested in something more. Who said I'm interested in anything?"

"Anyway, I'm just telling you, if you want a soul-mate, I know the best way to get that, scientifically tested and proven. It should appeal to your logical mind."

"You go ahead and tell me."

"It's simple. For a normal guy, I'd say maybe seven years after your first fuck, or until you're twenty-five, whichever comes first... but you know, a guy your age, and as serious as you are about S·M·F, you're a late starter and too busy for women most the time, so I'd say... twenty-six. Until then, you have to get with as many women as you can, as many as you have time for. And I don't just mean hoes, and I don't mean just for sex. Get to know them, get to even care about them. But not too much, because you're going to have to break up with every one of them."

"But what if I find a really excellent one—one that seems just perfect? Or one I just don't want to let go of?"

"It don't matter, that's part of the formula. You got to break up with her."

"Why?"

"Because you're inexperienced and you don't know it, but you probably going to find someone better."

"Okay, but..."

"Look, the thing is, after all this, you reach the magic number. For you, that's your twenty-sixth birthday. After that, you're in the next stage of the game."

"What do I do then?"

"Same thing. Get with as many women as you can. But the difference is, now, if you meet someone who's better than anyone you got with before, I mean better than *anyone*, then she's the one for you to stick with. You'll know it."

"That's pretty cynical."

"Don't worry, you get a lot of adventure along the way, and a lot of play. It's not all calculating, but it's still a winning strategy."

"But what if, after all that, I don't meet someone better?"

"That happens. It happens a lot actually. You miss the boat, it's your tough luck, but I'm telling you, having no strategy gives you much worse odds. Almost everyone today winds up unhappy in love, miserable, alone or in a bad marriage, or hooked on too long with the wrong woman, dissatisfied, envying, getting disrespected. Or you could wind up like so many of our fathers, sticking around long enough to try to make it work, failing, and leaving kids behind. Avoid the kids until you've found the soul-mate."

"There's always accidents."

"Just don't spooge irresponsibly. But if you follow my strategy, many guys would wind up with a good woman, maybe not a soulmate, but better than what they would have settled for otherwise. And I bet maybe one out of three guys wind up meeting they soulmate and staying together, total winners. I'm telling you. My uncle was that kind of guy, and he wound up with my aunt, and it's been all good for them. And I got with an older woman once, she followed the same kind of strategy until she met her perfect man at about age thirty, and she was really happy about it."

"If it worked out so well for her, how come she got with you?"

"She had a different kind of bad luck. He died."

"Guess you can't calculate against that."

"Nah."

After our conversation, I thought a lot about what Flower said, and I even used it as something to teach the babies and new-recruits when it became appropriate. But as for my own life... honestly I've never been the romantic type.

13.

"WE'VE ACTUALLY GOT an excess of cash," Lettuce reported. "I'd suggest we issue a dividend."

"Why is our money not making money?" Jonas asked. "Just circulate; get it back out there."

"Well, the demand for loans is just as high as always, but we been backing off some customers. We've had two defaults this month, and it's looking like we can't give much credit to some humans. There's one guy—Thunder, Too-Tall, and One-Time had to take him for a drag in the river and put a debtor's scar on him."

"How much did he owe?"

"Three thou'."

"And?"

"We'll get it, but not quick. He got no job, and I think his kin would let him die."

"And who's the other defaultor?"

"This guy Julius who borrowed somewhat regularly. One of Dancer's marks. He was reliable, and then all of a sudden Dancer heard he gone for police protection. He don't step out, but where he thinks is safe circumstances, he tells humans that if something happens to him, the cops know who to look for. Almost bragging, actually."

"How much he owe?"

"Nine hundred."

"Fucker's willing to risk death for *nine hundred dollars!?* That don't make sense."

"Cloud," said President, "we got serious problems. We haven't settled things with Jack-Rabbit Lubbs yet, and now we looking like we can't manage debt."

Thayne said, "We're working on solutions, but right now we got to hold down the fort. Maybe Lettuce is right, though.

Let's issue a big dividend and keep the troops satisfied. We'll raise cash in other ways. Mala?"

"Yeah," I said, "that all sounds fine, but it's more than obvious we need to get some kind of justice for Coca-Cola sooner than later. This is going on too long, and the troops are really aching to take meaningful action. Not just scrapping or playing defense within our limited count."

"Giddy down, Mala," said Jonas.

"Why?"

"Because I'm telling you, things'll get handled."

"And why am I not getting involved in the planning? Fact is, I told you we should have acted when Rashed Macklin got head-flown down at the Skizz Club. Lubbs are one captain down, they're vulnerable, they're getting ready to trip over they own laces."

"But they know where the danger is coming from. I'm telling you, they'll be cracking in a matter of weeks, but the timing has to be right."

"Jonas, the timing *was* right..."

"Screw down."

After a respectful pause, during which the rest of the room was silent, I answered back briefly: "Anyway, you've heard me."

Jonas turned to Lettuce: "Don't issue a dividend."

Amazin' asked, "Not even a little one like last month?" He wasn't an O.G., but his trust level was high, so he'd been assigned to quartermastor.

"None. Salt it. Thayne, stick around. Everyone else, keep it screwed till you hear otherwise."

Seven hours later, at about five AM, Jonas woke me up along with the other guys who were sleeping at the clubhouse that night. Waking up to see him was like getting squared; his clothes were filthy with blood. But when we all rubbed the sleep out of our eyes, we gathered for the story.

"Shit happens quickly, motherfuckers," said Jonas. "The kid who shot Cola... he's over with."

We leaped up. "Yeah!"

"I had to kill his brother too."

We were shouting and jumping, grabbing Jonas and each other, and celebrating, even though we didn't know yet how it fell out.

"I'm sorry, I owed it to y'all to get you involved, but I only found out how to get to him yesterday."

We were thrilled.

When we settled down a bit, he gave instruction.

"Alright, bring in all the boys from wherever you can find them. Get word out what happened, and then we got war planning to do."

Young and Rootwork were the only soldiers on hand, so they went out to gather the troops. Then Jonas talked to me in particular.

"It was just a few hours before our meeting I found out. The motherfucker was Lee Budhu. I know you suspected him earlier, and you were right. He was bragging around about being the shooter, but only yesterday, thanks to hoes' talking, I got a call about where he'd be, at a brother's place outside the count."

"But you just went on a word you couldn't trust—no confirmation, no real plan?"

"Listen. There's times to think, but there's times to not think. I know. But if I'd talked to you about it in the meeting, worst thing could happen, you'd put a doubt in my mind."

"And if you'd walked into a house full of Lubbs, or if the police came around..."

"Honor trumps cleverness."

"Yeah, yeah."

"I couldn't talk to you. But don't worry, you'll have a lot

to think about now. You got mad honor, for sure, but for *my sake* I think you'd be too cautious to let me stick my neck out."

But how did he know that, when he never gave me the chance?

"If I offended you, it was unavoidable," he said.

This incident is how I learned the power of stubbornness.

When Sammy came in, he shouted "You are successor!!" and hugged Jonas and the celebration picked up energy again. And when most of the other boys had arrived, Jonas speech-ified a bit.

"You've all been strong, and it's time to get stronger. I want to say thanks to Amazin' for his B&E skills; he got me in the house even though he didn't know why..."

"But when I heard the screaming, I soon found out."

We laughed.

"And thanks to Proven for his excellent driving skills. What else?"

Thayne said, "Well, I think we'll have a little more free-dom to act. Turns out L and P are not getting bail. They'll be down for years."

"Cool," said Jonas. "So, we got any business going on today?"

Amazin' said, "Thunder and Hardcore got some cars to rob."

Bank said, "And I got some collections."

"Nobody else?"

"Sure, we got games to play," said Fierce. "I was going to send Ace downtown again to run some chuck-a-luck."

"No, fuck the usual stuff. Get the robbing and collecting done quick. Everybody else is on vacation today."

"And Horseback got the plate out his wrist. He's coming out the hospital again."

"Good, bring him in to party. We can knock him around to keep the doctors in business. Lid off tonight. Tomorrow, usual business, but be on the ready to move at any time."

"Cloud, you're our hero, man."

"Cool, cool. And, oh yeah, Solid, you gotta stick around for a little conference. Mala, we'll have a chat upstairs, and then O.G.s join us. Everyone else, take care of big business, take a nap, or take a hike until like four o'clock."

"Clouuuuud!" That was Sammy shouting for no particular reason.

⁂

"L and P" were Lloyd Harris and Phil Green, two Black Steel Nine O.G.s who'd been taken in for an armed bank robbery. We hadn't had any open conflict with the Nines in a long while, but we never knew when things might change.

"I think with they new troubles the Nines are less likely to break the peace, so we should be able to get business taken care of. But I don't know," said Jonas. "The equation's more complicated than that."

"Well, shit's always complicated," I said. "What's the problem?"

"You know the Jack-Rabbit Lubbs are ready to fall apart if we just ratchet up the pressure. But we can't be sure... if some of our boys get wounded or nabbed by the cops, the Nines could still rush in on us. And we going to have serious negotiation problems with the Grogans no matter how things fall out. They think of the corner as Family Of Man territory."

"True, but they fantasy's not going to become a reality. They hungry to expand, but if we crack the J-Lubbs, how much conflict are the Grogans going to want to withstand?"

"Maybe not much, but we can't fight everyone. One war after another is going to wear us out. As far as our troops know, I'm not going to tell them there's any limit on our strength, but you know and I know... we don't know how many casualties we can take, or how many months of fighting we can bear. That's what's got the Nines so fucked up despite they early strength and despite everything. They been warring on and off for years."

"So the answer is obvious."

"You think so?"

"Yeah. We just take the war to the Nines first."

"Our beef is with the Lubbs."

"Fine. But the Nines been, honestly, the scariest mother-fuckers in town for God knows how long, and now they on the verge of collapse. Let's push them over the verge. Once that happens, Lubbs will have no heart to resist. And the Nines... everybody hates and envies those motherfuckers. They've warred with the Grogans, they've warred with Los Asesinos, they've given us some heat..."

"Well, we gave it to them..."

"True. But once we eliminate them, everything falls into place. We don't need no business across the ocean long-term. So we pull out and let the Grogans eat up like half that territory, while we turn our attention to Jack-Rabbit corner and our own neighborhood."

"That's... yeah. That sounds like a plan. But then, I got something else going on I gotta act on quickly."

"What's that?"

"Mesmer found out where Warren Jeanpierre takes his girlfriend sometimes on the weekend." (Warren Jeanpierre was an O.G. in the Jack-Rabbit F.O.M., and Leroy "Mesmer" Mosely was one of our wannabes.) "He and some of the other babies were out fucking around at Grover Beach when they spotted him. Now I hear the Grogans have been looking for Jeanpierre and he may be in hiding. So I want to send Solid and his crew on a beach vacation, with instructions that if Jeanpierre shows up, they're to kill him."

"Sure, that sounds cool. But also, you should send Mesmer with. If he wants to be a soldier, there's no point in him creeping around looking at humans; he got to act."

"True."

"But I still say be ready to move on the Nines A.S.A.P. Maybe simultaneously."

"We can't split up our force."

"I don't mean at the same time, I mean around the same time, like within days. Like as soon as they get Jeanpierre, or if they can't get him quick, bring them back and move before the Nines have a notion we looking at them. Meanwhile, you know... strategize."

"Yeah, that's all helpful, we'll talk about it with the O.G.s and work shit out. And I'm getting Solid on the bus with his boys tonight."

"Okay, that's business. Now, Jonas... you alright?"

"Huh? Yeah sure."

"I mean, you don't gotta front with me. Seriously."

"Yeah, no problem. I'm cool."

"Alright."

�

Around this time I had been having a really scary dream of a white-painted concrete cinderblock wall—pretty much every night—but that night I slept well, with no dream. This seemed strange to me, and I talked with Thayne about it in the morning.

"What do you think? I have the same dream for like eight or nine nights at least, but then after Jonas kills Budhu, I sleep fine."

"You're relieved. Obviously you can sleep well; we finally fixed things."

"Yeah, it seemed like it should be something like that, but I don't know. I don't think so. It don't feel like relief, just... blank. It means something. But I don't know what."

"If it's not a good sign, then it's nothing at all. Dreams is just dreams. I mean, I don't want to disappoint you if you think this is all serious, but it's in our waking lives we live or die. The rest—even scientists haven't figured that shit out."

"How you know they haven't figured it out?"

"No one's given me an explanation that made sense."

❧

We put in two days of strategy meetings to work out the best ways to move against the Nines. Ultimately, our best plans were simple but audacious and relied mainly on using numbers and surprise to target a few leaders in the heart of they own count.

Then Solid and his team came back from Grover Beach with Warren Jeanpierre's body.

14.

Solid and his boys checked in at they hotel on day one, then split up to visit or eat at some area restaurants. They also took turns cruising up and down the beach with they eyes open. They did they job not really expecting to find Jeanpierre or any other Lubbs. Early on day two, though, Toothless spotted Jeanpierre lounging on a beach blanket with his girlfriend.

Rollup was off somewhere prowling hotel lobbies, so he missed the action, but the other boys got together and acted immediately.

Humans on the beach, if they noticed, reacted with laughter or surprise at first—like they were witnessing a prank—when they saw five guys sprinting onto the sand with balaclavas over they face like ninjas, covered in black clothes from ankle to wrist, wearing gloves. And then the team fell on they target with hunting knives before he knew what was happening. They kicked his girl around and slashed her face when she fought, and left her screaming for help—but no help came—while they ran off the beach carrying the still wriggling but dying body wrapped in the blanket. They left nothing behind but some bits of potato salad, sandwiches, a couple of bottles, and blood stains soaking the sand.

The crew changed clothes in the van while driving away. Rollup would have to find his own way home. After that, they abandoned the vehicle with knives still in it, on a quiet suburban street, and they transferred the body to the trunk of another car they used for the escape. After a quick ride into town, Solid dropped the guys off in two groups to travel by bus and train, while he drove the rest of the way on his own. He didn't meet any traffic stops.

After we got the report—after the bags of clothes, the blanket, the bloody gloves were burned, and the escape-car got ditched—Jonas told us to hold off on attacking the Nines for one extra day so we could display the body in Jack-Rabbit Corner. I was assigned along with One-Time, Toothless, Young, Mesmer, Too-Tall, and Rollup, while Solid was given the night for R&R.

As Jonas instructed us to do, at 3:30 in the morning we brought Jeanpierre's body to a corner just half-a-block away from where Leeshawn Lavant was living. One-Time, who knew how to hoist, went up a short ladder to reach a permanent steel step on a telephone pole about ten feet up, and he hung a pulley. We quickly got Jeanpierre's body out and tied it by the left foot, then we hoisted him upside down and tied off the rope on a spike Mesmer hammered in near the bottom of the pole. We hung Jeanpierre upside down because Jonas told us never to hang a man by the neck; it looks too much like a lynching, and we don't want to conjure that image.

We took a good look at him, dangling in his crazy awkward way. I thought of the blood stains on the sand the boys had told me about. I tried to visualize, and I thought, *Maybe someday, somewhere, a kid will dig on the beach to make a sandcastle, and he'll find, just a few inches below the surface, the whole beach for miles around is soaked in blood, deep, deep down to the bedrock. You never know; it could happen.*

We drove off and made for the clubhouse.

15.

"ALRIGHT, IT'S HAPPENING," said Jonas. "No one's been robbed on Thomas, Ducasse, or Dorsey, or in the whole area from Belle Isle to Berrigan or Silver down to Yost in more than a year. No drugs been sold openly in years. As for selling sneaky, well... I doubt it. Civilians is safe. Kids around here don't pick up hooks... they moms don't encourage them even to play with toy guns. And when bullets fly, they targeted mainly at us. But we don't dodge. We got heart like lions. We still have neighbors look at us like bad influences, but most would get behind us. Most know the situation is cleaner and better. Now we gotta stick our necks out."

"Fuck yeah," said Thayne. "This is not a time to sit back and count our money; we gotta fucking prove we can earn our stay on this fucking earth."

"We had our fun, and now it's time for some deadlier games."

"Strip Monopoly's more my style," said Sammy.

"Well you can stay home and play by yourself."

"Nah, you know I'm going to come back from the fight covered in more gore than anyone—Black-Steel-Nine intestines hanging out my mouth. If anyone loves to commit violence in the name of humanitarian purposes more than I, I'd like you to show him to me."

"Anyway, everyone can fight this fight for they own purposes, but we also have a united purpose to establish dominion for the S·M·F. There will be no contesting our will when it comes to living our life, our way, in our own count. And we define the terms."

"You know it," Solid said. And the boys agreed.

I led a group of twelve, including soldiers and a few wannabes, with Fierce by my side, as we rushed into the Corner Pocket Pool Hall on Merchant and Via Luna. We met with some friction at the door, but we cut everyone who got in our way, and we came on like a storm, fast enough they couldn't resist. We knew there'd be Nines there, but we got luckier than we expected: they generol, Kerry Nettles, was on site. Ace recognized him right away, and the boys moved in, and while some enemies were jumping out windows to escape—there was no other way out—Nettles started blasting with a hook he'd got ready, probably as soon as he heard us rushing.

Suddenly all the energy went out of me and I crumpled. It's a crude description, but I just became a sack of pain. You could say I struggled for breath... I had the panic... but it wasn't a conscious struggle... everything I did and felt was like an involuntary convulsion that went on for an indefinite time. Now I've lost my sense of that time. But I feel as though some part of me was permanently trapped in that moment. I had this internal thought: *I'm here too. I matter.* When I think of it, I feel very sad even though I really don't know why. I don't remember moaning when I got shot, but I guess I did.

"You fucking flopped around like a fish, man, with blood at the gills." That's all the boys will say about it nowadays. Jelly likes to razz me, but not in front of others. He respects my honor.

But the attack went on, and business got taken care of. The boys killed Nettles. On our side, Dancer died of a head wound. A few blocks away, Cloud's team caught four Nines soldiers in a car and surrounded them. Lettuce and President brought they boys too, and they killed two. One escaped, and the last of the four survived his wounds.

Also seriously wounded on they side was an O.G. named Andre Nesbitt, and a couple of other soldiers, in a fight Efrem's team started on a corner outside the All Nite Diner on Ridge Avenue, on the eastern extreme of the Nines' count. Efrem got scuffed up too, as did many of the boys, and Horseback got injured again, this time from a chunk of wood split his scalp when a guy beat him over the head with it. That fight went on for a long time, the cops broke it up, and Efrem, Jelly, and Clip got jailed for a short spell until Lettuce bailed them out. Nobody testified against them, and the fight was they alibi, so they couldn't get blamed for killings elsewhere. Nines got jailed and bailed too.

The boys delivered me to a Jewish hospital outside the city had a reputation for good food. They didn't want to take me to Drew Memorial or Saint Luke's because they thought they'd get arrested on the spot, and maybe I'd get connected to the Kerry Nettles killing—but that was a little kooky because I nearly died. And the cops came out and interviewed me anyway soon as I could talk. (I said nothing.)

The bullet that got me passed through my chest and out my back, so there was no ballistic evidence in my body—but I don't think they could subpoena a bullet anyway. Nothing came to nothing in all the investigation that ensued. The only one who got surely connected to a murder was Dancer, and he was dead.

Market had a legitimate reason not to participate in the fight (soon known as "the massacre") because he was in jail for being stupid. He'd got caught in a burglary. Thunder and Knockdown, on the other hand, were supposed to be there. (Thunder!? Who could imagine?) They never showed, and that was it for them. They dissolved like smoke.

"They worse than dead," said Thayne. "Cookie fought for us, babies fought, but those two punks vanished? We're not going to talk about them, and we don't have to justify anything on they behalf. Goodbye."

So that was our loss. But we were growing. Leroy "Mesmer" Mosely was made soldier right after the Grover Beach killing, and now he was fully respected as a veteran. And after the fight, five other wannabes got made soldiers for participating, after they passed they tests: "No Love" Barry Love, King "Slice" Holmes, "Dangerous" Malcolm Jones, Eric "Cruel" Robinson, and Paul "Quite-Right" McNeal.

I was the only one who missed Dancer's funeral, though. By all reports it was a sad affair. A lot of guys said Dancer was the wrong one to die. Many would have been happy to die in his place, or so they said. I wouldn't go so far myself. I'd come too close for me to ever envy the dead. But it's true, he was too good to go out like that. Too good a man.

When my mom looked at me in the hospital, it was pretty painful. I could see the conflict in her eyes. But just in case I didn't get the message, she told it to me straight: "Should I say goodbye to you now so I can skip your funeral? I don't want to lose another person in my life. But maybe you're already long gone."

Mom cried a lot more than I expected. I don't remember her being that way when I was younger. Since I'd come out of juvie, we hadn't had many fights. I think she saw the futility of it. Generally, I came and went when I wanted, and if she hassled me, or if I wanted a more positive outlook, I always had the clubhouse or other places to crash. And even though things were awkward with us, I was glad she'd found a way to cope and resign herself with the way things were. She didn't become one of those delusional moms like many do, telling lies to theyselves pretending ignorance. She didn't become the enthusiastic super-supportive mom either. Rather, she was sort of a saint to me because she kept on with her life, kept on getting on that bus to work, didn't deny me as her son but didn't deny the truth about my lifestyle. And from the early days when I was getting money, I'd tried to buy her a few little presents here and there, and she always said "thank you" and put them away. Never used them. So I decided to stop throwing money down that hole if it wasn't appreciated and just caused embarrassment. But I didn't expect to see her cry so much to see me hurt. It was fucking awkward.

16.

IF I'D HAD INSURANCE, I'd have stayed in the hospital longer, but without it I was out in five days. I camped out at Jonas's place so no one would think I was retiring. But I wasn't well enough to get involved in any new fights for a while. I couldn't imagine running half a block, and even going up three steps was hard. The pain pills helped, but they also made me light-headed and confused.

It was important S·M·F move quick because we didn't want to give the Grogans a chance to get the jump. And Jonas wanted to wait to negotiate with them *after* making a move in the Corner first.

The Grogans were seen putting out feelers on the fringes of what had been Nines territory. They'd held off during the funerals because it was illegal to murder or assault while a click was celebrating a funeral, but now they started posting soldiers to test the streets.

At the same time, rumor said Leeshawn Lavant was missing, and humans believed we had already killed him. But we hadn't. So we figured he went into hiding, and this made the opportunity we were hoping for.

Jonas sat by me at night when I was having some trouble sleeping.

"You always resting whenever there's big action to contemplate," he said.

"What rest? What is that?"

"I'm just razzing you. Rest up."

"I'm telling you I don't know what that means."

"Heh… So, you hear what happened to One-Time?"

"Oh, God, what?"

"Don't worry, nothing serious. It's just funny. That guy Julius been dodging Dancer so long not to pay his money, One-Time got the idea to settle with dude right away because he so mad over what happened to Dancer, right? Like this Julius guy is responsible for everything."

"So, what's he going to do, though?"

"I'm telling you. I said don't fuck around with that right now, we getting ready for more serious business in the corner... You know, everyone's all emotional and shit, and we're at a turning point, but One-Time, he won't hear it, he goes out and finds Julius's dad because no one can ever find Julius when we're looking—beats the man down in the street. Now, with what we done already, no one wants to fuck around or get the police involved—like, we already ruling these streets with authority. So, today, a guy we don't know walks up and hands a envelope to a baby who delivers it to One-Time. Payment, finally, for the debt."

"Cool. And?"

"And one bill is like—how can I say?—crusty."

"Uhh..."

"And Julius is already going around bragging he jerked off on the money!"

"Oh, my God. That is sick."

"Seriously. Did you know people could be so...?"

"What gets in people's head sometimes? I don't understand."

"Not everyone thinks as clear as you and I, Mala. Anyway, we're going to have to do something about One-Time."

"A cleansing."

"Sure. How?"

"I think... I think, if he literally washes his hand in Julius's blood, that'll do it. Until then, he should probably sit out on any action."

"I could use him tomorrow."

"I wouldn't."

"Meanwhile, I guess he's going to have to deliver that money to the bank using tongs!"

"Heh, yeah. And, so... have fun."

"Sure. I'll give you all the details. But this is the last time you sit out on a fight, alright?"

❧

And the next night, Jonas mounted his cloud, thunderbolts in hand, to sail forth before his nation.

They moved on the Fuck Club.

❧

Things went smoother than smooth. When more than twenty guys marched up to the entrance, there was no resistance. Jeff Hargrove, they captain who ran the business at Fuck Club on most nights, could have pulled a weapon, but he didn't. He opened his office, came out with his empty hands in front of him, and said, "Just give me a chance to run." He got his wish. Hoes said he was a gorilla pimp with more heart to beat a woman than hit a man and no heart to put his life on the line.

Jonas oversaw the triage when we broke up they stable. Workable hoes we kept for a few days to trade to the Grogans. The ragged ones got cut loose; we told them stay out of the Corner, permanently. But the choicest ones got set aside. We sent them to Gandara for Los Asesinos to work. Hoes made noise, but there were no serious objections.

One girl though, Lexie, she got special treatment. She was Keychain's sister, and we sent her back to her mom with instructions to stay out of the business. We called it a "rescue," and Keychain was required to send her an allowance for a few months to help get her straight. We warned her we'd be checking up on her too.

Cash got absorbed into our treasury. The few ounces of product we found got pitched in the water the next day off the end of "the beach." We got a workable ho to carry it because a taboo prevented us from touching it.

Boys laughed a lot about a moment when, an hour into they raid, a cop peeled down the street with his siren going. Turned out he was hassling some guy smoking on the corner half a block down. Cops had been kept away from the hoeing business so long they didn't investigate to know what was going on that night.

✒

Lavant never showed his face again, and stories went round saying he'd disappeared with money owed to his soldiers, so the unity of the click was shattered.

There was one O.G. who was serious about trying to stay in business in the Corner even after the Fuck Club fell. That's Nolan Eason. He sent word out he'd shoot to kill if anyone fucked with his business on Ulrich from Freya to Osbourne. In doing this, he sketched out a tiny strip of what had been Jack-Rabbit-Lubb territory. But he could hardly expect to keep it together.

Meanwhile, Jonas, Thayne, and President finally met with some Grogan O.G.s in a downtown club, far from the action, to negotiate a peace. That went smooth as well, mainly because we were negotiating from a position of power and Jonas was generous. He shipped them the hoes we'd captured, free of charge, and we made it clear the S·M·F had no interest in muscling into the business north of Silver Ave. In return, it had to be understood the Fams had no business in Jack-Rabbit Corner, our count was expanded, and they were not to give aid or comfort to Nolan Eason now he was trying to oppose us. If Grogan Fams had beef to settle with surviving Jack-Rabbit

Fams or Nines, that was theys to settle. And ditto for us, we'd take care of our own work.

As Grogan Family chief Calvin Trice said, "We got no problem with any of that. Our vision is to the east, not south, and if we get no static from your direction, we happy to go on peaceful like we always have."

They treated Jonas with respect, and Jonas got proud over that, considering Calvin was twenty-eight and a twice-convicted felon whereas Jonas was still a teen and just getting started.

❧

We didn't face any serious reprisals from the Nines, and we suspected they couldn't mount any. They were under-siege on all sides and facing financial ruin, while they rep was in tatters. No juice. They couldn't put dealers on the streets without getting shot at, and couldn't poke they heads in any local bars or clubs without seeing angry Grogan Lubbs glowering at them. They'd hardly had the funds for the three funerals they held, and not many attended. And Phil Green was in prison now and trying to claim Generolship from inside, but not many were listening to him on the street, while his most trusted friend, Lloyd Harris, had checked-in after turning evidence in court.

Nolan Eason was bigger trouble than we'd expected, but we knew there'd be trouble *somewhere*.

While we were making a serious effort to try to clean up Jack-Rabbit Corner, which was pretty much ours, without detracting too much from our usual business (and while allowing some fun time too for the boys—I mean, we need our fun!), we had to cross Ulrich Street routinely, and we didn't want to show any respect for Eason's ultimatum. No shots were fired, but there was a few scuffles, and whenever the Lubbs disappeared, they always popped back up again later.

I was up and around by this time, not quite up to full

strength, but able to let my face be seen walking about, and able to oversee some of the action.

There was a whole section of abandoned housing occupied by squatters. The Lubbs used to make racketeering money by collecting rent. We took the opposite approach to business by contracting ourselves out as agents to the landlords who were willing to pay us to evict squatters from they building. It was just too tough for them to get them out legally. Some of the squatters were Baby-Man Ronins, the new masterless and dispossessed remains of the former Jack-Rabbit Lubbs who couldn't find employment in Eason's set. They didn't really have the heart to stand up to us, and they moved when we moved them. Solid got shot at once from a distant apartment window, but the shooter or shooters vanished. Other squatters were mostly bums. There was only a few legit poor families which we didn't like having to push out, but frankly they were not in a good situation where they were. We hoped they'd be better off moving somewhere else.

Civilians were hostile to us, even though we were there for the good of they neighborhood, and we knew if deadly violence erupted we couldn't count on humans to stay quiet about it if the cops asked questions. On one Ulrich-Street crossing, when Young, Clip, and Rootwork responded to threats with they fists and a brawl broke out, cops broke that fight up and cuffed everyone after knocking them around for a while. Some of us arrived too late for action and we were only able to stop the cop-brutality by shouting and menacing the police. Young and Clip got charged with concealed weapons for the knives they carried even though they hadn't used them, while the Lubb dealers couldn't get taken on drugs because they didn't have product on they person. And all the while the arrests were happening, one old hag on the corner was shrieking, "They the ones hung Warren Jeanpierre! They the ones. Fuck the whole neighborhood up; got kids scared to sleep. Fucking murderous bastards need to be took down or took out!"

We knew that lazy old fiend was just hoping we wouldn't cut off her supply, like she couldn't walk four or five blocks to buy from the Grogans. Half of us wanted to cut her tits off. Jonas maintained the peace.

17.

Jonas met with me for a one-to-one chat over steaks.

"How we doing, Mal?"

"We? We doing alright."

"Give me details."

"Our neighborhood's cleaner than ever. No product on the street. Of course, still in the houses maybe, but maybe less."

"I told you we got that problem already solved."

"A few of the neighbors don't always appreciate us."

"Who says what about me don't matter to me."

"We got North Brehms locked up except for Los Asesinos territory, Walden, and Carthage, and Nolan Eason's still giving us a pain in the ass. The boys are otherwise happy, having fun, housed and fed. We get love and we get respect. We live our way."

"And?"

"And nothing."

"And we're killing humans. You noticed that, right?"

"Come on, you getting philosophical? I'm not that type."

"No, you come on. You gotta be that type. You're wise."

"I'm just good at saying 'Do this, don't do that; that'll work, that won't.' I'm pragmatic. You're our soul."

"No, I don't accept that responsibility. You got your own soul. Don't tell me you don't think."

"What I got to think about?"

"Look. Let me teach *you*, then. Memory is very important. Never neglect that. We don't cloud our minds because you gotta be attentive. Be aware, and remember everything."

"I guess."

"Live life knowing you will look back on it. Make it something you can look back on. But that requires attentiveness. That's the only way you're going to see there's good in what we're doing. To do that, you gotta see there's evil in what we're doing too. Those don't come apart. Are you able to sacrifice something even of your spirit—your own morals—knowing it serves something higher?"

"We take care of our own."

"Exactly. But that don't diminish the fact we do harm. We gotta recognize and be conscious of the choices we make, with posterity in mind. Compromise is done consciously; it's not compelled. We're under pressure, the duress is constant, we can't step out of the reality of our situation. But our situation don't make the decisions for us, we do that."

"Yeah, okay, I think I know what you're saying. But I don't have any trouble with it."

"That's fucked up. You gotta have trouble with it, and then you have to work out that trouble. Otherwise you're going to be the one that's hurt by the thoughts you never thought. Don't forget man, I'm a thinker. I don't hide, and I chastise myself for the harm I do. But you're sometimes failing to be my conscience. When we're alone, I mean, the two of us. Don't fall down and let things become routine."

"Alright, so like, you want me to criticize you."

"I want you to start by criticizing yourself. In doing that, you become the conscience of the S·M·F. That's *our* spirit."

"You laying a burden on me. But I honestly didn't know you were this philosophical."

"You entrusted me without knowing me? That's an error on your part."

"You're not going to knock me off, are you?"

"Shut up! We're not the Mafia, bitch. You're my boy."

"Cool."

I went to bed that night, not thinking about what Jonas said so much as thinking about the Mafia. That's when I came upon my idea the Mafia don't exist, and they never did. Believe me, depending on who you are or where you from, that can be a profound realization. Oddly, it's only in retrospect the substance of what Jonah said came to have meaning for me.

The words became a part of me without my really... listening. Life's weird like that.

18.

Jonas, I, and the other O.G.s, plus Solid and Too-Tall, marched up to the building where we knew Nolan Eason spent most of the day (when he wasn't overseeing things on the street). Boys came in and out the basement there frequently, so we figured it for they main base of operations. We confronted three of his boys sitting on the stoop.

"Tell Nolan we want to see him."

"He's not here."

"Tell him."

"He's not here."

"Like you can't find him. Alright. We'll be here tomorrow."

The next day at the same time, it was me, Jonas, and Too-Tall only. Since they knew we were coming, we couldn't risk all the O.G.s getting caught out at once. We were met by an anonymous Afro, probably a captain.

"What you want?"

"We're going down to Warton Field Courts. It's neutral and public."

"Hardly neutral. Fucking Fuerza runs out there."

"Sometimes. Anyway, it's way outside the count, and we don't have any dealings with La Fuerza. We'll be there at three."

"What the fuck do I care where you go?"

"Just tell Nolan he can pick a spot out there, or nearby, or whatever, to parley. We don't really give a fuck where, actually. He can invite us in his kitchen if he wants."

Dude didn't reply, and we didn't repeat ourselves.

We went out to Warton Field Courts and watched some basketball. Dancer used to play out there sometime before he got embroiled in S·M·F business and got dead, and the friends he used to play with had moved on and got hooked up with a different click. Not hostile, but they didn't have a common ground with us or too fond a memory of Dancer anymore.

Nolan Eason never showed up, and he didn't send an envoy.

19.

PRESIDENT AND I got together a plan for a recreational outing with a gambling theme. We decided to take some of the boys out to the racetrack to bet on horses. Not everyone could come, but we got together a kind of cross-section of guys from the various teams, captains and veteran soldiers. All together there was like ten or eleven of us, including my road-dogs Efrem and Fierce, plus Terrible, Flower, Jelly, Ace, Hardcore, and Cookie. And one other guy, I don't remember who.

None of us knew shit about horses, but it was a chance for us to blow off some steam and probably some money like a bunch of fools. I tried to do a little research before we went anyway, and some of the other boys asked questions and read racing forms.

"There's no beating this game, though."

"So it don't matter who we bet. We can pick any horse."

"Well, I don't know though; I'm still going to try."

"Basically you *can't* play smart, but you *can* play stupid."

"What do you mean there's no beating it? I heard there's professionals."

"There's no professionals. I mean, there's big winners who *call* theyselves professionals, but actually they just the luckiest suckers going."

"They know the game."

"The biggest professionals own the horses."

"Or breed them."

"The biggest *betting winners* have plenty of knowledge, for sure. But they also have a big box of luck."

"For three years at a time? Four years? A lifetime?"

"Even a lifetime isn't very long in this game. How many bets you think you can make in a year? How many thousand-dollar bets? The serious horse players make so few meaningful bets, you can write it all up to variance."

"Yeah, whatever."

"That's like saying I can beat this game today by dumb luck too."

"No it isn't."

"Hey, I got guys who beat my sports book regular—and more power to them as long as I can balance it. But there's experts who can bet better than I could."

"We still get the paper."

"Don't matter, they playing to beat four-and-a-half percent. At the track, we gotta beat *seventeen percent takeout*. That don't happen realistically. And that don't even count the breakage."

"Fuck man, what the hell is breakage?"

"Brain's been studying."

"Call it extra pennies coming out your pocket."

"I don't care about pennies."

"Fuck you don't. We make our living off pennies, just like the state politicians."

"*You* do. I make my money off the mintest fucking vees. No penny scraper."

"And you can lose it just as fast."

"Damn right."

"Anyhow, I heard it goes to put kids through school."

"Hell of a lot of good school did us."

We all went our own way in the betting. In the first race, I liked a horse named Patwin if I could get 5-to-1 or better, but it never got close to that on the toteboard. I made a token bet for fun at twenty dollars getting 7-to-2 because I didn't want to pussy out on the first race. Some of the boys followed my lead, while President and some others preferred a 10-to-1 dog called Eyes On Prize. None of us picked the favorite, Debby's Rascal, which went off at 1-to-2. Patwin came fourth, three lengths behind the winner, Debby's Rascal, who led wire to wire. Eyes On Prize was third. Jelly was the only guy to collect money because he made a place bet on the number-two finisher, Quasar. He felt pretty clever for that shit, but we rode him hard enough nobody made anything but win bets for the rest of the day.

"What are we supposed to look for when they walk the horses out... you know, in this place here?"

"Some kind of energy, I guess."

"Paddock."

"I don't know, I think it's like when wine drinkers take a little sip at the restaurant before they drink a glass."

"Yeah, that's not my culture."

"No, but it's simpler than you think. Like you think they being sophisticated and making an informed judgment. *Oh, there's a little too much fruit in this Chateau La Tour. Where are the cinnamon and leather overtones?* But really it's like *Does the wine suck? Is it spoiled?* No, seriously, that's all it is."

"So, like, if the horse isn't hopping around here on a broken leg then he probably going to win."

"No, but just look to see who you would disqualify. Like, does one look too jumpy, or it don't respond to the jockey or something? Or sweaty."

"Maybe sweaty balls are bad."

"There's no horse out here like that."

"I don't see any balls on them."

"They're not goats!"

"You know what a gelding is, right?"

"Well then, we're not going to learn in one day to read horses' minds."

"I have a hard enough time trying to read a bitch's mind. And they're at least human."

"Maybe."

In the second race, everyone was making fifty-dollar bets or more. I put a hundred on Pen and Ink, which went off at 6-to-1. President and his faction went with a 2-to-1 pony named Epicure. This time Efrem got lucky when his 9-to-1 pick,

Extended Play, came from fifth place out of a pack four-wide at the top of the stretch to steal the lead on Pen and Ink—who'd been front runner for the first seven furlongs in the one-mile race but lost steam at the end. It was Extended Play by a head, and Efrem's fifty-dollar ticket turned into five hundred and ten bucks ($20.20 for $2). Epicure got lost in the crowd: fifth place out of seven runners.

"Now I know what a chuck-a-luck chump feels like."

"True."

"Hey, we just getting started, man."

"Yeah, by the end of this day, you'll be so shit upon you'll know what a Tijuana toilet feels like!"

"Here come the beans!"

In the third race, Efrem's horse literally died in the gate. Modern Mummy reared up, threw his rider, and broke his own neck. Efrem thought he'd lost his two-hundred-dollar bet, but the horse got scratched and his bet refunded. After a long delay while they hauled that corpse out of there, the horses went back in the gate, and they were off.

I had put eighty dollars on the even-money favorite, Ship It To Shorty, and most of the boys, including President, followed. Only Flower and Hardcore favored the 4-to-1 horse, Center.

We all lost our shirts when the long-shot Art Of Victory came in at 25-to-1. The rare individual in the grandstand, here and there, shouted in celebration, while the rest of us tossed up a blizzard of losing tickets.

"You want some more beer?"

"Don't buy any more beer, man. They more strict about carding at the beer stands than at the betting windows."

"Just send Ivan again. With that scrubby beard he can pass for forty."

"You should put some grey in it; maybe you could apply for social security."

"Anyway, it makes us conspicuous."

"Like we don't stand out. You feel at home here already? The regulars ain't looking at us like we a walking scandal?"

In the fourth and fifth race the bloodbath continued and none of us collected a dime.

"Whose idea was this again? Seriously, who?"

In the sixth race we all went crazy and fell in love with a name. The six horses on the race card were Shore Fershootin, Fancy Lad, Onion Eater, Sleipnir's Grani, Fetlock Holmes, and African Zulu.

"We got to bet African Zulu!"

"Why?"

"African Zulu!"

"Come on. He's not even that good."

"He's only... look, came in fourth in his last race, a sixteen-thousand-dollar claim, and now he's running a twenty-thousand-dollar claims race. Why they stepped him up?"

"Fuck if I know. But dude here in the recommendations says 'African Zulu might surprise.'"

"Heh. He also calls Onion Eater his 'best pick!'"

"That's only if Onion Eater got better than 4-to-1. Look at the board. Everyone's betting the 'best pick.' He's only 2-to-1. Probably get 3-to-2 when they run."

"So what? African Zulu's only 3-to-1."

"Fuck the numbers, look. His last race was a fluke. African Zulu does well at shorter distances, he has a good record at six to seven furlongs. He won three of his first four starts."

"Against horses with no class; this is a different level of competition."

"No. Look, his owners put him in a sixteen-thousand claim at a mile and a quarter, and he still didn't do bad. His fourth place finish was only one length behind the winner. Now his team's got him back in at a comfortable distance. They believe in him, and I do too."

"Bullshit, you don't know horses! You just like the name!"

At this point I was ready to go crazy with the rest of them, and even though I agreed the odds didn't look good, I said, "Fuck it, I'm betting four hundred on African Zulu."

"Cool. President?"

"I'll match that."

We all went nuts. Every one of us put whatever we could afford on African Zulu to win. Efrem, who was still up a little from his second-race victory, decided to make it five hundred, and no one went for less than a hundred.

President made another stipulation. "Alright, you all bet as much as you want for yourselves, but I think we each have to put up an additional thirty bucks on behalf of the click. Thirty dollars each; cough up, and I'll buy a team-S·M·F ticket for the boys."

"Smart money" came flowing in just before the race on Sleipnir's Grani, which became the 5-to-4 favorite. Onion Eater remained 2-to-1 and African Zulu was 7-to-2. The longest of long-shots was Fancy Lad at 60-to-1.

Bell rang, gates flew open, and hoofs churned soil. Fancy Lad stumbled and was quickly left behind by the rest of the pack, but it was otherwise a hotly contested race, with Onion Eater holding the lead for the first three furlongs. African Zulu was a few lengths behind on the outside. Sleipnir's Grani pulled ahead of Onion Eater slightly as they neared the turn, making it Sleipnir's Grani, Onion Eater, Shore Fershootin, African Zulu, with Fetlock Holmes trailing three lengths behind, and Fancy Lad limping along somewhere near the aft horizon.

At the turn it became a clusterfuck against the rail, too much traffic, while African Zulu opened up and stole the show, finishing half a length ahead of Sleipnir's Grani, Shore Fershootin, and Onion Eater, each within a few inches of each other. They had to do a photo finish to check second and third place, but we knew who the winner was.

The excitement was mad, and we were chanting "African

Zulu! African Zulu!" as we went to collect our winnings. On the way, I noticed a disproportionate number of happy black faces coming out of the crowd, also to collect. And some of the old-timer white bettors also saluted us with amused smiles near the windows.

We didn't stick around for races seven, eight, or nine, and went home big winners. Efrem had the most individually, but we all had something, and we had something for the crew too.

"But we played like suckers," I said. "We absolutely should not have won."

On the way home, we spent some of the money off the team-S·M·F ticket to buy Italian sausages, hamburger meat, buns, beer, pickles, whiskey, American-cheese slices, charcoal briquettes, and cigars to celebrate with the whole click, and we handed out the rest of the click's winnings in twenty dollar bills to every soldier who came to the roof-top barbeque. You best believe the lid was off.

That same week, I finished my first four-mile run on the treadmill at the downtown Bronze Fitness Center, and I got completely off the pain-pills. Life was looking sunny and bright.

20.

With Nolan Eason it became a castle siege. When it came to words, he was as belligerent as ever, but fact was he was in no position to venture any major hostility against us. We heard he'd been talking with some guys from the Carthage Street Family Of Man, but we didn't take it too serious. Carthage Street was its own faction kept to theyselves east of Brandywine Park, and they never gave us one ounce of beef. But some of the Baby-Man Ronins had moved out that way when we evicted them, which meant they could get incited to bring us trouble.

Jonas elected to keep things cool in our dealings with Nolan and avoid another massacre while the cops were eying us with mad suspicion. We acted just to starve Nolan out by harassing his customers. Soon they started buying outside the count. This went alright for a while, but we were at an impasse, and we resented the fact there was an island of hostility in our otherwise pristine count.

During the siege, Nolan was reduced to playing dominoes in his basement most of the time and smoking bats on the stoop with his boys. He was living on whatever crumbs he'd saved. And he was waiting.

Chatting with Lettuce one time, he told me Smooth and Rootwork were taken off the payroll because of several months of non-participation.

"They just don't come out to play anymore."

"What about that new guy, Quite-Right McNeal. I haven't seen much of him."

"He hasn't been too active. We're keeping an eye on him, but he on the rolls for now."

That's when I became aware of silent attrition. I mean,

rules say "S·M·F Brother—Brother for Life," but apparently "brothers" sometimes go in for early retirement.

❧

Maximum was still in with us, but he got hisself in a fucked up situation I'll tell you about later.

❧

Market went down for five-to-ten in the state pen. He didn't say anything against us, and we would have liked to help him out, but there was nothing we could do. So he became our first genuine convict. We wrote to him as often as we could, and visited him sometimes.

As is usual, the cops called him an S·M·F "captain" and "organizer"—when he was only a soldier—simply because they'd got him. If they'd nabbed me they'd have said I was the "leader" and "founder." The authorities always give you an unofficial promotion.

21.

"WHY we being so weak with Nolan, Cloud?"

We were having an O.G. council meeting.

"What's weak? Why do you say 'weak'?"

"We could kill him."

"Why, though? He's fucking annoying, I know, but why kill? Plus the cops are really looking to bust us on something—not like they fucking care, but you know they expect something to happen."

"So what? There's always opportunities."

"True. So, who's saying we should kill Nolan Eason?"

President was the one who'd suggested it. Proven nodded his head, and Lettuce raised his hand a little. I remained uncommitted, and Jonas noticed that.

Jonas said, "Well I'm against it. I respect the fact he didn't dissolve like Leeshawn and those other punks, Baby-Man Ronins and all."

Lettuce said, "But you know he's not respecting our law. He's not just sitting in that basement doing nothing. Did you know he was using pizza boys to deliver product from a place across the tracks?"

"I heard all you had to do is order 'special garlic sticks,'" said President. "Or say 'put some salt in it.'"

"So burn the pizzeria!"

"I'm sorry, Jonas, but that's crazy. It's outside the count, it's owned by some Italian dude, and fucker probably don't even know what his delivery boys are up to."

Jonas said, "But I don't know if it's morally right to kill Nolan. I don't."

Everyone looked at him, shocked, like, *Where's Sammy? Is this a joke?*

President responded. "I don't know what to say to that. But look what you've already put us through; I mean think of

Solid, and think of Thayne right here. We all got blood on our hands. Why should Nolan stick his thumb in our eye, and we can't do shit about it? Am I right? Someone speak up?"

I said, "I don't really know what you getting at, Jonas. But I figure we do have to look at every situation differently... like what we did in the past may have been necessary..."

"Anyway, we're at war here," said President.

"Exactly," said Thayne.

"I know you think otherwise," said Jonas, "but war is when morals count most. Just the time when humans think morality to be out of the question is when the morality of our decisions have the most effect. We going to set the tone for how we handle *our own*. This isn't a violent intruder. We in his home now."

"And he's a big fucking pest. You wanted to clean up the corner. He got to go."

"But he hasn't crossed any lines, really. He has his rhetoric, and we have ours. But ya'll need to be flexible a little bit. Am I right, Mala? What do you think? No fence sitting."

"I'd love to see you pull this off non-violently," I said. "But I don't see any way. You just have to think what it means to the click. No one wants it to be known we can be patiently abused, you know? I mean, do you know something we don't? Some special way of working this so we don't get burned and we can still hold our heads up?"

"No. I don't have a magic solution. But time will tell."

"This is fucking weird man," said President. "Jesus Christ. Thank god the soldiers don't sit in on some of our meetings."

We ended laughing at the absurdity of it, but I respected Jonas's capacity to surprise us at every step. And where the fuck *was* Sammy?

22.

WELL, WE SAW SAMMY the next day when Jonas, Lettuce, Amazin' and I returned to the house from a beach outing with Bank and his team. Sammy was sitting by hisself on the sofa, not watching TV or anything, just sipping whiskey at two in the afternoon.

"Roses, bitches. Smell them."

"What the fuck, Sammy? Where you been?"

"Three days vacation. You know I earned it."

"I ain't say you didn't earn it," said Jonas, "but I don't like disappearances sometimes."

"Why you watch me so close like a jealous lover?"

"What!?"

"Come on!"

"Nah, I'm just saying, I'm not going anywhere when times is as sweet as this. Look around. We got it made."

We all settled down, except Amazin' who fetched us some beers from the mini-fridge in the corner.

"We do got it made," said Jonas.

"Damn straight," said Sammy. "We got half-naked ghetto-rats riding they bikes in lazy circles, no shirts, torn pants, few prospects. Boarded up windows, empty lots, garbage in the streets, dry dust everywhere. Rusty topped cars thirty or forty years old with bald tires parked on every corner. Old shoes hanging in the wires. Warehouses. Row houses. And old humans living in basements, peeking out behind curtains, wondering when they going to get shot."

"Bullshit. The one thing humans know around here is, if they stay inside the law, nobody gets hurt."

"But in this land," continued Sammy, "we're the kings." He sipped. "And don't mind the old humans' suspicions. They don't mean any harm, like I don't mean when I tell you. They safe here, for sure, but in they minds... y'all know from experience, right? Once your eyes have seen..."

"Shut up."

"Once your eyes have seen certain things... Death is fucking coming man. So, I'm not kidding, these are the good times now. These are the good times."

Lettuce switched on the TV now, and he and Amazin' resolved to let Sammy be Sammy. But I was listening, and as usual, Jonas was giving him all the latitude he wanted to be an asshole.

Then, after a while, Thayne came in with Hops and Ace.

Jonas shouted when he saw Thayne, "Hey! We got enough O.G.s in the house to carry a resolution."

"Where's president?"

"We don't need him. Effective immediately, Sammy loses the title of Jestor. All in support?" He held his hand up.

Sammy immediately sat up, upset. I, Lettuce, and Thayne quickly raised our hands. Amazin' raised his hand too.

"Put your hand down, bitch!" shouted Sammy. "You're not an O.G.!"

Amazin' put his hand down again, but the rest of our hands remained in the air.

"Motion carried," said Jonas."

"But..."

"Screw down Sammy."

Sammy immediately complied. I'd never heard him so quiet.

"But who's going to be Jestor now?" asked Hops.

"I nominate Thayne, a.k.a. Proven, to the honored position of Jestor," said Jonas. "All in support?"

Lettuce and I raised our hands. Thayne looked bewildered, almost as shocked as Sammy.

"So, now," said Jonas. "Stir us up with your words, Thayne. Or sing, or something."

"I. Fuck, I ain't some clown."

We all laughed except for the two victims.

"Motion to immediately strip Thayne of the title of Jestor and return it to Sammy?" said Jonas.

Our hands immediately went up.

"Hah, hah!" shouted Sammy, and he leapt to his feet. "That's fucking right. Lid off. What you think Thayne, you think you can carry my burden? I'm higher than a Muckamuck."

"Motion..." said Jonas.

Sammy stopped short, terrified.

"I'm just fucking with you," laughed Jonas.

"Jesus, kid. About to give me a heart attack."

23.

IT WAS AROUND THIS TIME we had to ostracize Maximum. Maximum was a good soldier, and none of us were sure how to handle him. Fact was, we had never had to kick anyone out the click before, and we knew we had to make the consequences pretty dire, but none of the O.G.s really wanted to make him suffer too bad. We had sympathy.

The fucked up situation began with some razzing within the click. Ever since Maximum's buddy Knockdown had run off at a critical time, some of the soldiers took to dissing Maximum, saying he was unreliable and he might run off too. Even a couple of the newer recruits, Slice and Dangerous, tried to puff theyselves up a bit by shitting on Maximum's reputation. I'd had to violate Slice myself one time with three face-slaps to try to squash it. Maximum was not permitted to take personal revenge because Slice apologized and declined a fight-offer. That should have been the end of it.

Then Maximum, one day, while walking riverside somewhere out of the count with a couple of babies and a girl of his, ran into his old buddy Knockdown. Maximum jumped him immediately. Problem was, Maximum got hisself knocked out. Badly. Publicly. In front of everyone. The babies jumped in, knocked Knockdown around a bit, and ran him off, but Maximum's pride was critically wounded.

When the story spread within the click, Nap approached Maximum to try to calm him down—tell him to stay cool and ride it out for a while. But Maximum squared Nap and drew blood from his nose. Nap and Maximum both fought bravely until we broke it up.

That was it for Max. It was an absolute taboo for a soldier to spill the blood of another soldier, except in an officially sanctioned fight sponsored by an O.G. or captain. Even seniors rarely bloodied juniors, and then only in the case of serious violations—the one exception being Jestor had special disciplinary privileges.

Jonas said to me, "I know what you thinking, right? Fucker just got unlucky."

"It happens," I said.

So we had to excommunicate him, and the only way we could think to do it, without being too cruel, without killing him, but ensuring a fear of death, was to pitch him off the pier at "the beach."

On the drive out, he kept telling us, "I can't swim."

"You'll learn," said Thayne.

We took him out the car naked, with his feet and hands tied, ran along the edge of the train rails, handed him over the fence, then ran him out along the pier. Nearby, two white boys saw us and ran off.

As we were getting out further on the pier the panic was rising, and he soon started screaming.

"Put him down, put him down," I said. We put him on his feet for a moment. "Get the ropes off." We untied the ropes. He was shivering, and when we lifted him to take him to the end he started struggling and screaming again.

"It don't make no difference, I can't swim!"

We pitched him in, head first, but he rolled in the air so he fell on his back. He came up sputtering and choking on what he'd swallowed, but he got out a few words.

"Really, help!"

"If you were drowning, you couldn't speak!" shouted Thayne.

"I'm going down!"

"Fuck, he can swim. Does he look like he's going to die?"

"He don't look happy."

"Let's go."

We started to walk away, but when we got off the pier, I got up close to Thayne and tapped him.

"I'm going to hang back and help him."

"I didn't hear you say it... Take a smoke break. I'll see you later."

Thayne and the boys got in the car, and as they were driving off, Mesmer threw Maximum's pair of pants out the window. I ran, grabbed them, then ran back to the pier.

As I was approaching, I saw Sammy come out of nowhere (he hadn't come with us), and he also started walking out along the pier, carrying a coiled rope. I guess he had a heart. I caught up with him.

"I got his pants."

"Fuck the pants, let's get him out the water."

At the end of the pier, I saw Maximum was mostly submerged, but he was clinging fiercely to the slippery, splintery wood post propped up the pier. He was only maybe five feet below us. I figured his balls and chest were getting scratched on barnacles.

"Jesus Christ, boys, don't let me die here."

Sammy lowered the rope to him, but Maximum hesitated to grab it.

"I can't."

"Just grab the fucking rope."

He tried to grab it, but lost his grip on the pole, splashed, and the rope slipped out his hand. The rope was some kind of plastic or nylon, and pretty thin.

"God damn," said Sammy. He pulled the rope up, then tied a loop in it somewhere near the end, and dangled it again. Max had struggled his way back to the post.

"God damn, help! Don't kill me! Help!"

"Shut the fuck up, alright? Don't bring the police out here when we trying to save your life. Now get your arm through that loop. Get it! Don't just look at it, you don't get many chances. Go!"

Maximum got his arm through the loop while struggling, his face went under, but Sammy pulled up a bit, and Max got his other hand on the rope too.

"Just hook your elbow, and grab that loop again with your left hand... alright... Mala, help me haul this bitch."

We tried to pull him up, but he shouted in pain and wriggled too much as we lifted his body like 80% out of the water, and our feet were slipping—the rope too because we couldn't grip it well—so we let him down to where he was half-submerged.

"Let's just haul him to shore."

We ran along the pier, pulling the rope, half-suspending and dragging Maximum through the water until he shouted again:

"Rocks!"

And we stopped.

"If your legs are on the rocks, you can stand or crawl your way out," Sammy said, and we dropped the rope. I threw the pants down in the shallow water beside him.

"Don't let us see you again," I shouted, and Sammy and I ran back away from the shore, towards the fence, the rails, the street.

"You're a much better man than I gave you credit for," I told Sammy.

"And you're a bigger cunt than I ever thought," he said.

Then it was up to me to deal with Knockdown. He couldn't be allowed to get away with what he done. But none of us still wanted to kill him, so I took Efrem's old advice. When I found where Knockdown was hanging, after three weeks of asking questions and posting babies on the lookout, I ran up on him, beat him with my fists, and when he was down, I stabbed him in the gluteus.

Then we were done with the two made too much trouble.

24.

AFTER HANGING OUT with Efrem and Heaven and eating sandwiches, we went back over to Jonas's place to meet up and go to the movies. Most of the click were going that night. When we arrived, this ho Tanya was arguing with President. She was kind of wobbly on her feet, and President was telling her she couldn't stay in the house when we were out.

"Come on," she said. "I done... Come on. I just had sex with all of y'all, man, you can't let me stay for a few hours?"

"Who?" President said. "Who you had sex with?"

"All of y'all, you know."

"Really?" President pointed at Too-Tall. "What about that guy?"

"Well, not him, but most of you guys... like six guys, man, come on..."

"What about me?" asked President.

"No, I didn't have sex with you."

"What! Are you kidding me?" Everyone was laughing now. "You don't even remember!"

"Well... I just closed my eyes and I'm drunk man, I don't know!"

"No you didn't! Hah... did you really think you had sex with me?"

"I don't know, like I said, I'm confused..."

"Who had sex with this girl?"

Rollup showed his hand with a sheepish look, and so did Quite-Right.

"Guess a few of us...," said Quite-Right.

"See, I ain't lying."

"Don't matter. No hoes in the house when the boys out."

"But not everyone's going. Come on, I can just watch television or whatever."

"No, we're going to the movies. You want to come with? You can come."

"Well, I ain't fucking in no movie theater."

Altogether there was over twenty of us walking, so we went up to Silver and walked west across the bridge. As we were walking along on the south side of the bridge, we saw six guys walking back from downtown on the north side. They threw up Grogan signs. In response, some of our boys picked up bits of garbage and shit and tossed it across the street, shouting "Fuck all Lubbs!" Most of the trash just fell on passing cars, and the Grogans kept the peace and kept walking. They didn't want to fuck with us in a serious manner.

When we got to the theater, we met up with those who drove, including Jonas, Thayne, Solid and some of his boys, and Sammy. Two of the babies who were most desirous of being made soldiers had come out way early and bought tickets for the whole click in advance, in case they sold out. Only problem was they got only twenty-five tickets, the show *had* sold out, and now there was twenty-nine of us. So that meant the babies were going to have to sit out, and two more of us too. President immediately told the ho Tanya to fuck off.

"No, it's not fair, I just walked all the way over here!" She looked like she was going to cry.

But Quite-Right played the gentleman.

"That's alright, Tanya. Take my seat. Go ahead and have fun."

"Are you kidding me?!" shouted Toothless, almost angry.

"I already seen it. I already seen it," explained Quite-Right.

"That's cool," said Sammy. "But who else, then?"

Jonas said, "Mala, you choose."

"Me? Why me?"

"You the Brain."

"This the fucking kind of assignment you use the Brain for, eh? Fuck. Alright..."

I looked around. I was half-tempted to pick Sammy just for spite... or maybe even Jonas hisself to see how that would play. But then I had a grudge against Bank I had to settle, so I called him and Slice out.

"Alright. Bank, Slice, get over here."

"Why?" said Bank.

"Because you fucked up that robbery. You shouldn't have left Slice out there by hisself to get caught."

"He didn't get caught."

"Don't argue."

I took one of the tickets, ripped it in half, and gave one piece to each of them.

"Get over there outside the end of the parking lot, beyond the lights, and fight. Whoever comes back with both halves of the ticket gets to see a movie tonight."

"But I can't fight him," Slice said. "He's my captain."

"I'm saying you can. And after today, if you beat Bank, you go over to Solid's team. We probably shouldn't have you working together anyway."

"No, no, I got nothing against Bank."

"Well get ready for the nut-crushing then, because Bank don't back down and don't go easy on no one. I've spoken."

I turned to Quite-Right.

"And because you got nothing else to do, you can call the fight. But don't break it up too quick; if I don't see bruises on the winner, I know y'all were just fucking around."

Nine or ten of us went in to get our popcorn and seats, while most of the boys were more interested in watching the fight instead.

The movie was some typical Hollywood mainstream bullshit about jewel thieves, supposedly based on a true story, called "Star of India." They made it into a kind of comedy and updated it so the FBI could have science experts and helicopters and shit. In the first ten minutes the heist was played out where the supposed expert thieves steal a bunch of diamonds by smashing open the cases in a museum using squeegees the janitor left behind.

"They should make a movie about us," said Fierce. "Seriously. You think stealing diamonds is hard? Remember when Horseback and Flower stole a *refrigerator*?"

"That's what I'm talking about."

"Serious crime!"

"Shhhhh!"

Some humans were shushing us.

Now some of our S·M·F brothers started trickling in, back from the fight, and word went around quick the cops had busted up the fight.

"Who won?"

"Nobody. They bashed each other's faces for a while, then the cops broke it up and now they out on the curb in cuffs."

"Them plus Flower."

"Speak of the devil."

"Why? What he do?"

"I don't know, he was just watching, but I guess he argued when the cops told him to move or something."

"Should we go out and help?"

"Fuck," I said. "I guess I'll go and offer moral support."

I got up and made my way out, while the rest of the crew were ambling in, mostly laughing. Among the guys coming in was Quite-Right, who held the two halves of the torn ticket and flashed a wicked grin.

"Haaaa!"

Sammy shouted, "You are ticket holdor!"

Quite-Right shoved Hardcore aside so he could sit with Tanya.

Outside, I saw Bank, Slice, and Flower, with they heads

down and the cuffs behind they backs, with the cops marching up and down behind them with flashlights shining on them.

"Hey!" I called, "I'm going to send Lettuce down, alright? To bail you out if you need it."

"Fuck you Mala," said Flower. "You knew the cops just circle this place every Friday."

"Don't talk," said a cop, and hit Flower on the shoulder with his flashlight.

Another cop walked up in front of my face.

"Move off," he said.

I backed away but waited until they put the boys in the squad cars and drove off—which took like eight minutes—and then I went in to watch the rest of the movie.

When the show was done, Lettuce went to the police station to see if anyone would be held, or if bail could be paid off the schedule, or if they would have to attend a hearing. As expected, no one got booked; they just chilled in the station for a couple of hours and then got released without bail—which I found out the next day—but meanwhile we had the rest of the night ahead.

Everyone kind of went different ways after the show was over. Most of the boys went back towards home over the bridge again. Others drifted this way and that.

Jonas threw his arm over my shoulder: "Mala, my boy, we gotta go to James's and drink some godfathers. Lettuce, you want to come?"

"Nah. Thanks. Say hi to Uncle James."

"Thayne? Prez?"

"No. We don't like the pace of that joint. It's club night."

"Serious?"

"How about you, Mala?" asked President. "You don't have to let Jonas drag you off to that old ladies' place."

"But I'm kind of partial to the godfathers."

❧

"James's" was actually a bar called "Gordan's Knot," and Lettuce's Uncle James worked there as bartender most nights. He was an oldschool gangster in retirement from the days when the Bullwhips were big downtown. Nowadays, they were mostly unheard of. Uncle James always hooked us up without ever carding us. He also upgraded us from Johnnie Walker to Laphroaig, and even though it tasted kind of crazy at first—kind of like a burnt Almond Joy—it soon became my favorite. I even dreamed about it.

"In the next life, we gotta call ourselves the L.G.C.," I said. "Laphroaig Godfather Crew."

"You dreaming again."

"What you mean 'again?'"

"I don't mean it like an insult. I like it. You showing imagination."

"And?"

"I don't know. It's familiar, like from when we were kids."

"I don't remember."

"Well, anyway, you keep that imagination going. You don't gotta run on automatic all the time."

"I wouldn't say I run on automatic."

We just sipped and looked around. I found myself thinking about... old wood.

Jonas said, "There's so much possibility in this life, you know."

"You think so?"

"Sure."

"And what you think is possible? I mean, you want something? What?"

"To be a proud and noble black man."

"Huh. In the world today? I don't see it."

"Come on."

"I don't even know what that looks like. I mean, the first thing I picture is MLK. He was a true noble warrior."

"True."

"Fearless and wise. He accomplished great things, and... and he got his head blasted and then we still wound up exactly where we are today. And to be honest, I know the evil shit he was combating was truly evil, but really I don't think Jim Crow would even change my life a whole lot."

"Come on, now."

"It's not like I spend a lot of time at the soda-fountain sitting next to white guys and they wholesome white daughters."

A quick look around confirmed my point.

"Sure, sure," said Jonas. "But on the other hand, some of the things you done, you could have got yourself lynched back then. But today... Well, also, if you wanted your slice of that pie, you could have gone to college."

"Coulda woulda."

"We don't know how life looks like from that perspective, when you're not embattled all the time."

"So could you, you know. You could have done that."

"Heh. Looks like we opted out." Pause. "But also... I feel good about the choices I made. I don't know how you feel."

"I'm not the person to ask."

"I know that."

A quiet moment.

"What you think Bank's thinking right now?" Jonas asked.

"*Fuck Mala. Fuck Mala. Fuck Mala.*"

He laughed.

"Got any ideas lately?" he asked after a while.

"Nope. Well, yeah, actually... First of all, your approach to Nolan Eason is pretty crazy, but meanwhile, what the fuck he up to? I'm starting to think he just a straight-up coward and we done over-respected him for nothing. The other possibility is he got some kind of deep plot, but by now I'm leaning towards the idea he just stupid."

"Alright, let's say he stupid."

"So I say he dissolves and we forget him so long as he don't have any community support, and I think most his boys have abandoned him already. You get your way, in other words. Non-violent resolution."

"Second?"

"Huh?"

"You said 'First...'"

"Oh. I do like the direction you're going. I mean, whatever you do, you do with confidence, and the boys look up to you and follow without question. I mean, I think the notion we're more than even a family; we're a movement—that's catching on."

"It better catch."

"You right. There's no real rivalry, except maybe petty squabbling from time to time, as long as the boys have outlets, you know. But we O.G.s, we gotta have a notion where we going sometimes. And we don't always know."

"Be honest. Do you think Thayne doubts me?"

"Not for a second. And he's no rival. He's the most solid, loyal guy going, for sure."

"Does Lettuce doubt?"

"No. He's not that deep, but if he hears doubts he echoes them maybe."

"And President?"

"He's just President. He's a thinker, but he the same he always is, you know. He don't doubt *you* in any essential way, he just likes to talk and see where talking gets him. Or, I don't know, but he's no one to worry about."

"So then that leaves you."

"Yeah, well I... Well, fuck! You know, you always want me to ask questions and challenge you, so yeah. I don't know what the fuck you doing actually! What are you doing, and why?"

"I'm doing the same thing I always tell you, up front. I'm no deeper than the surface I've shown, you know. I don't know everything. But I take steps, you know, one at a time. I don't know where it's going, but I do my best."

"That's bullshit."

"You think I got a master plan."

"Well you fucked me on the Lee Budhu thing. I still remember that."

"I didn't fuck you, I just didn't tell you what was happening. But I understand. That gave you the false impression I got everything in hand. I don't. But I'm trying to take steps in the right direction is all."

"You got secrets."

"I don't."

I started to feel very angry inside for some reason. I don't know if it was the alcohol which got me buzzing in no time flat, but it was warm in my nose and throat. I think I hadn't spoken strongly to Jonas in a while, and it was getting me mad.

He went on. "Believe me, I'm really a lot like you. And you're like me. I'm just telling you... you can carry the weight of this world if you have to. Even if, you know, someday, I'm gone."

That hit me.

"Don't say that," I said.

"Did you hear Gandara bit it?"

"Yeah, I heard. Who did it?"

"Don't know... His brother Jorge came to repay a final debt

to me. To us, I mean. So I told him maybe I'll go to Gandara's funeral. You know what he said?"

"No, what?"

"'Family don't want no black at the funeral.'"

"That's fucked."

25.

ONE TIME Jonas and I were walking in the corner, just surveying the scene, when we heard some guncracks out in a narrow alley behind an abandoned warehouse. We heard occasional shots before, but this was close, so we walked over to see what was happening.

Some kids of maybe twelve years age were shooting at chalk circles drawn on a section of wood fence.

Jonas shouted. "Hey!"

The kid who was shooting stopped, looked, then looked over to his friend like to say *What the fuck?*

Jonas was stern. "What you doing? No hooks in the corner."

"Who you?"

"What's that in your hand?"

"A .25."

"Give it here."

The kid hesitated.

"Give it here."

"Why?"

"I told you, no hooks in the corner. Don't make me say it again."

The kid walked over, then placed a little nickel-plated thing in Jonas's hand. Jonas held it flat in his palm, not even touching the trigger guard with his finger or wrapping his hand around the grip. He looked at it like an ugly, contemptible thing.

"You kids Ronins?"

"No."

"You looking to shoot a Boulevard?"

"No."

"You want to fuck with the S·M·F?"

"Hell no. We don't mean no disprespect, but sometimes a guy gotta look out for hisself, you know?"

"You kids just fucking around and you know it."

He handed the pistol back.

Take that and get rid of it somewhere, somehow. I don't want to see or hear it again.

"O.k., you got it."

The kid stuck it in his pocket and backed up a step, but then looked Jonas in the face somewhat defiantly.

"What do you want, kid?"

"Hell if I know."

"And you think you a man already?"

"Yeah, I'm a man."

"Why, because you strapped?"

The kid took the hook out his pocket again, and threw it over the fence into the weeds surrounded the railroad tracks.

"I don't need that shit. It's like you said, we just out to fuck around."

"Cool. Have a good day."

We started to walk, and sure as shit, the kid shouted, "Hey!"

"He going to try to get recruited, right?" said Jonas.

"Word."

"Why else he throw away a four-hundred dollar hook?"

"He just going to climb the fence and get it later."

"True."

We paid him no further mind, and kept walking.

26.

BARBECUE DAY IN THE PARK: it was a hot day and we were down at Fidelity Park, out in the woodsy part where there's grills and benches and spaces to lay out blankets and shit.

Efrem wasn't with us because he'd got shot in the legs, hip, and gut, and then jailed. He'd got entrapped in a police raid at an Association garage where we did business. Nap and Heaven went down with him too. The way the whole deal came out was a cop infiltrated the Association—he'd been with them for years—and just before busting the main target, Reggie Fegan, they waited for some of our boys to come in with hot vees to fuck us too. Association guys were strapped, bullets flew, Fegan put up a fight and died, and Efrem was just mixed up in it. Nap and Heaven got busted before the shootout while they was waiting outside away from the action. We lost $35,000 worth of cars along with the three brothers locked down, and a major source of revenue dried up since we didn't have a good place to sell anymore.

But we weren't in the park to whine about all that because it was barbecue day.

Some boys had girlfriends with them, and there was other varieties of claimed bitches too. There was some common hoes with us. But we didn't make any trouble out there and it was all clean fun.

Some white families were in the park. The first few to arrive in our corner of the woods kept apart. They preferred the spots put a little distance between them and us. But then a smallish family group came and parked at the bench right across from us. Two moms, two dads, five kids including a teenage daughter.

We raised our cups and shouted, "Happy barbecue day! Hey!"

They called back, "You too. Have fun!"

"Respectful humans," Jonas said.

The temperature between the sun and shade was like ten degrees difference. There were occasional breezes. Meat was cooking. It was nice.

"Hey, what you eating?"

"A sandwich."

"Nah, nah. Put that fucking sandwich down."

"Why?"

"I saw you eating a sandwich in the car coming over. Did you see anyone else eating?"

"No."

"So wait like five minutes. You'll get a burger like the rest of us."

"But I'm hungry."

"I didn't fucking wrap up all those sandwiches for you to eat half of them before the rest of us eat. You put the damn thing down."

Some of the boys were in a sunny, dusty clearing throwing a football around because they couldn't sit still, but soon they came back panting and thirsty.

"Is there anything to drink but beer?"

"What, like liquor? It's too early to get wasted."

"No, like fruit juice or something."

"Yeah, we got punch."

"Cool."

"Who's for rare, and who's for well done?"

"I'm for now."

"Man, I still remember I came here like eight years ago with my mom and dad and my sisters. It was nice, but Dad bought the chintziest hot dogs, I'm telling you. And the neighbors' grills: oh my God! That smell got me."

"That's why I like life now, I'm telling you."

"True."

"I feel like I been pretty lucky though. I mean, sometimes I didn't feel like I had much to keep me going."

"I hear that. Me too. Like, there was times I felt like I never really had any options going, you know? I sincerely don't remember feeling like there was any options. And, I don't know. The luckiest thing happened is I fell in with the S·M·F. I mean I fell in. I'm hard enough, it's not like I don't deserve it, but I don't think I really *earned* it, you know? Things just went that way."

"Don't even use that word 'deserve.' Proven goes nuts when he hears it."

"Damn straight."

...

"What up with you, Flower? What's got you down?"

"Don't ask."

"What."

"Ah… I'm having trouble collecting a debt, and it's pissing me off."

"Don't tell me. You loaned money to a woman."

"Hell, no! I don't mix business with pleasure."

"Uh, oh. Boys is going to talk about girls again."

"No we're not. I want to talk about this bitch that borrowed my money."

"Giddy down, though. We here to have fun."

"What's better than winding up Flower when he's steamed?"

"I'm telling you, this Afro's so meek and mild, you'd never think he'd renege on a debt."

"Who?"

"You know that kid Ronald I been telling you about."

"Oh, him!"

"He the kind of mainstream sucker sips Riunite on ice…"

"That's nice!"

"… on the weekend with his girlfriend…"

"She a virgin."

"... He wears the same polo shirts every day with the same crocodile on them..."

"Size: Extra-medium."

"... and he walks around with his ass-cheeks squeezed so tight they could crack walnuts..."

"They do."

"Am I right? And that's the bitch, he going to tell me 'I just can't pay right now'? Come on!"

"Hey, I don't like that word, you don't have to talk like that. You know there's ladies present."

"Shut up!"

"Calm down, Flower, we having a good time."

"So, have a good time! Who's stopping you? I'm a gentleman, I don't insult the ladies, but when I talk about a *bitch*, I'm talking about a *bitch* owes me money, and that *bitch* is a man, so don't get all worked up about *language*. Shit."

"Seriously."

"You want to have a private time with a bitch away from the click, that's alright, but anyone who needs to be protected from *language* don't need to be around us is all."

"Shit, you crazy."

"You think your problems amount to something? Come on. Squeeze that lemon tomorrow. I want to relax."

"If it wasn't for all the ash and bugs around this place."

"Come on, bitch."

"Excuse me while I go piss my dick off."

...

"Anyone seen the Keys–Tabbs fight?"

"Yeah, I was with my cousin and we watched it on Pay-Per-View."

"Sweet fight, right?"

"I never seen a guy fight like Tabbs. He's a lunatic."

"Yeah, I was sure he'd be down early, like in the first or

second round. I thought, 'He can't fuck around with Keys like that.' But I was wrong, he hung in almost to the end of the tenth round."

"Word, Keys was taken out his fight. I didn't expect that."

"Right? He didn't know what to do with Tabbs's style."

"Still, Tabbs got paid for his cockiness in the end."

"What!? You guys thought that was a good fight?"

"Sure."

"Tabbs only got away with his 'unorthodox' style because Keys is a stupid gorilla. He only good at knocking out sluggish bums like hisself."

"Not true. What about the fight with Oseitutu?"

"That was a fluke. Shit like that happens sometimes."

...

"Hey, I been thinking."

"Yeah?"

"You know, scientists developed a seedless watermelon, right?"

"Yeah?"

"So, how come they can't develop a shitless dog?"

"Good point."

...

"Hey, where's Liz today? I thought you said she was going to come."

"Don't you ever know when *not* to ask a question?"

"Why? What's going on?"

"She and I are having problems."

"Uh oh."

"Like, she raises a fuss about every damn thing. I don't understand her at all. It's not even worth my time."

"Hey, listen, I'll tell you how to work it out. You need the right psychology. Once you got them figured out, you'll find 90% of all conflicts with a female can be resolved with eye-contact alone."

"Really?"

"Sure. And if that don't work, try jaw-contact."

[Laughter]

"Nooooooo. You did not just say that!"

"Jaw-contact. I'm serious."

"Ha!"

"Are you listening to what these *children* are talking about? I do not want to hear that kind of talk."

"It's a joke!"

"Nuh, uh. Do you not have a mother?"

"Don't take it there."

"Do you not have a mother? Or a sister? Some woman or girl that's important in your life?"

"A lot of women are important in my life."

"For five or ten minutes at a time!"

"They can cook me breakfast."

"Shut up, you ain't never had a breakfast but cold cereal no milk."

"She can pour it."

"When you talk about manhandling a woman, that's reality. That's not a joke."

"Well what the fuck is there to joke about if not reality. Reality's the funniest shit I ever heard."

...

The soldiers, the babies, the girls all mouthed off how they wanted, but it was all good. We O.G.s took it easy and mingled. There was something beautiful about that day and its simplicity.

...

"The problem with trying to do good in the world," said Jonas, "is all goodwill is abused. Kindness is a weakness that gets exploited."

"Jonas is turning cynical," said Sammy.

"No, I'm not. Because I'm going to tell you that's not an excuse. You just gotta do what needs to be done regardless."

"Yeah?"

"Yeah. That's the cost an idealist pays. Call it social friction. A large part of your substance, no matter what, is going to be consumed by waste and corruption. So... are you just going to give in and let it *all* go to waste? Or are you going to strive to see that some small part of it gets redeemed?"

"Sounds like you're making a bid to be named a saint," said President.

"I wouldn't mind a halo," said Jonas.

"I just don't want any devil sticking any pitchforks up my ass."

"Hey, haven't you heard the good news?" asked Sammy with a goofy, fake, tight-lipped grin.

"What's that?"

"There is *no God*! Now grab while the grabbing's good."

...

"You want another burger Mala?"

"I can't say no."

"Here you go."

"You're a peach."

...

We had a lot of beautiful days, and that was one of them.

27.

"Why you ain't followed on your promise to kill one of us? Barking's not going to scare us off."

This was Jonas's last attempt to parley with Nolan Eason. Eason and a small number of his set had come out to march around conspicuously after four months dormant, and we cornered them. But the negotiation didn't go well.

"Fucking don't try to butter me up, bitch. Why the fuck we talking? My law is the same fucking law I told you. You and your click back the fuck off or be ready to die, because frankly I'm ready to go."

"We bigger than you can reckon with, and your click is almost dissolved... who's going to back you up? Seriously. You have absolutely no survivability on these streets anymore. None. And that's the truth."

There were civilian witnesses around, and it was early evening, before sunset. Some neighbors were peeping out windows, others were sitting on stoops, and a couple guys were standing on the opposite corner. Much of the community had come together lately, and the sentiment had turned strongly against Eason and the old-guard. Everyone was thankful when he was not around to be seen. But now one of Eason's captains was open-carrying a shotgun like he was practicing for some militia exercise.

"You not the only one that's willing to die, though," said Eason. "I got my honor."

"Why should we will that? How about we try to be smarter than that?"

"You're a fucking joke man. You just want me to roll over."

He signaled his captain, and the dude lowered the barrel and pointed it straight at Jonas. That made us all pause, then the gunman lowered the stock and fired over our heads.

I shrunk a bit. Most of us froze, then looked to see what

next. Some of the boys had spread out left and right. But none of us had advanced, and the shooter racked his shottie before we had a chance to rush.

"Back the fuck off now, bitches!" he shouted, sweeping the barrel back and forth low, around the level of our thighs, while stepping back a pace.

But, before moving, my eyes went to Jonas to see how he'd react first.

"You the ones have to walk away," he said loud.

"Whatever," said Eason. He started stepping, and his thugs went with him. "You been warned, for sure," he said.

"No. You've made your last fucking gesture," said Jonas.

At that same moment, or sometime round about, about three miles away, a bomb went off in a downtown pool-hall-café. The patronage there was mixed—black and white. One O.G. from the Grogan F.O.M., named Oscar Charles, lost both his feet and got severely burned. Two of his companions got knocked unconscious in the blast and suffered serious injuries. Lots of humans inhaled smoke, had strips of skin peeled off they bodies, or got ruptured eardrums.

It took a while for the police to figure out what happened, but they eventually found the bomb was in a pool-cue-case that was left under Charles's table, and witness reports led them to a suspect, followed by an arrest. But before I or my brothers heard anything about an investigation, we were caught up in our own mini-Armageddon.

It was the Saturday after the bombing when whole flocks of Grogan Lubbs came rushing into the corner.

28.

"WHAT THE FUCK is wrong with us, Cloud? How the fuck we supposed to answer this?"

"You think if we had two or three hooks, we'd have any better chances?"

"No, but least we could take some of these motherfuckers out!"

"Shut the fuck up; your mouth is going to get us killed."

Jonas and I, Solid and Amazin', plus Toothless, Terrible, and Sammy were all caught in a tiny kind of back lot between a grocery store and townhouse, lying down under two trees that filled the space to overcrowding. Amazin' was the one hollering. He'd been shot in the gut, and Jonas had part of his right ear blasted off. We'd run down there after squeezing through a crack like a foot and a half wide between neighboring buildings partially blocked by a fence of iron bars. It was a miracle escape in itself, but there was no safe place to run.

Amazin' overstepped the bounds by criticizing Jonas, but his wound gave him license to mouth off a bit. He was in a bad way. I'd been pretty impressed to see him haul hisself over that fence in his fucked-up condition.

Some of us wanted to talk to each other, but we mainly lay there quiet for a while, each in his own thoughts. There was another, wider alley at the north end of the lot, and it headed out and around a corner, presumably out to the street. But bullets had already come flying up that alley, ricocheting off the walls.

There were shots and blasts to be heard all around, and shouting.

Somewhere out in the street, someone was calling at the top of his voice, "Give up Dandridge, or this whole neighborhood's getting torched!"

The voice receded a bit after some minutes, but the shouting never stopped completely. Then there were some screeches and motor sounds, and a loud crash... several gun shots... running... shouts and screams. It seemed like it would go on forever now.

After a while, Solid said to Sammy, "Funny man, do your thing."

Sammy got up, and walked alone down the mystery alley. He peeked around the corner and said, "Peek-a-boo." Then, "Oh, fuck!" and he came running back as several nearby shots crack-cracked, and as he ran towards us, two dark forms came running after him, one big, one small. We leapt up, those who were able, to face this attack head on, but then we saw the two runners behind Sammy were scared shitless. They were bystanders caught up in it, looking for a place to run like us. A kind of fat middle-aged guy, and a shortish lady maybe forty years old.

Sammy flung hisself back on the ground in the shadows of the tree by Solid's side.

Solid said to Sammy, "When I said 'Do your thing,' I meant make us laugh!'"

"You mean that shit didn't make you laugh!?"

"What's going on out there?" I asked the new neighbors.

"I don't know." The guy was winded. "They... someone drove out and ran over one of them. They screaming. Me and my wife... we were laying down in our car, hoping they wouldn't see us. Then there was the crash, and our car got bumped and scraped. We thought we could run, but they started shooting at us."

"Alright."

"Who? Who ran them over? Could be one of our boys."

"Could be, I don't know."

The woman said, "They shot the guys who ran them over."

Sirens sounded now—more gunshots—lots of running.

We had to rally ourselves to get up and see what the fuck was going on. Sammy, Jonas, and I now pioneered forwards into the north alley. We looked out towards the street and saw reflections of the flashing police lights off the dark walls, and not much else. We creeped forward.

Coming to the street, looking to the left, we saw cops with pistols and long-guns aimed past us, down the street. But looking to our right... there was no one there for them to shoot at.

A couple of cops were struggling with a guy they restrained on the ground, and one was kneeling on the guy's head. Another guy, very nearby, probably in the street, was groaning. We couldn't see him past the parked cars blocked our view.

Now a trio of cops came forward, one of them dropped out of sight—the groaning got worse—while the two others rushed towards a smashed up car in the middle of the street. They looked with they lights through the windshield.

"They look dead!" shouted one cop.

The cops flinched at the sound of shots on a nearby street.

They moved around, hooks ready, towards the passenger side of the car, opened up, and looked inside. Inspected the back seat too.

Then more cops coming down the sidewalk shined they lights towards our alley. They must have seen one of us move.

"Come out of that alley and lay the fuck down!"

"We just watching! We hurt!"

"Come out now!"

We came out almost immediately—Jonas pitched a blade back down the alley first, from out his back pocket—and we lay prone on the sidewalk, hands out on the pavement.

"We didn't do nothing!"

"Don't even tell them that shit," Sammy said low, "or they'll use it against you."

"Our boy's shot!"

The cops now got up close where they could see us clearly, and they kept us in they sights. Two came over, frisked us, rolled us over to check our crotches. One saw Jonas's head wound.

"Alright, sit up against that wall and don't move. Just don't move."

They circled us and checked us again more carefully, but holstered they weapons. They let us get up and move to the wall one at a time, then sit.

"What did you see?"

"Nothing, we just heard shots down around the corner and ran."

"Our boy is really badly hurt. He could be dying."

"Where is he?"

"Down in the lot behind the alley."

Cops looked at each other like *fuck that.*

"Just sit here and don't move."

The cops walked and talked to each other for a while. One of them talked in a radio. Some got posted to the end of the street near the corner.

"Help!" A voice called out. It was from back where we came from.

"God damn," said a cop. Then he walked over and shouted down the alley.

"What is it!?"

"There's a kid down here's been shot."

"Just sit still until we secure the area."

I realized it was the middle-aged guy who was calling out to the police.

"But he looking real bad. I think he needs help right away."

"There's nothing we can do right now. Don't move him until the ambulance comes."

"But don't you know first aid or something!?"

The cop didn't respond. After a while, he moved away.

Now only one cop was standing in our proximity, while the others were busy here and there.

"Come on, man, what the fuck?" said Sammy.

The cop didn't respond. He didn't seem comfortable.

"Are we under arrest?"

"You gotta sit still and let us do our job. There's guys out there shooting still."

"But what good does it do for us to sit here and let a brother die in the alley?"

The middle-aged guy came walking out the alley now, almost careless, with his hands up to show he was safe, but almost like shrugging.

"This is ridiculous," he said, "you all need to do something."

Cops came over and frisked him, then one of them walked into the alley to finally see what was going on.

"What's your name," Jonas said to the middle-aged guy.

"Sam."

We were sitting there for another ten minutes before the cop came out with Sam's wife, followed by Terrible, who looked out into the street.

"Oh man, that... isn't that Mesmer's car?"

We all stood up.

"Oh, God."

"Yeah, that's it."

The car in the street, diagonal across two lanes, with the windows all blasted out and bullet holes in it was Mesmer's. He'd bought the used dark-blue Nova earlier in the month.

We approached closer to where we could see the loudly moaning guy who was lying in the street. We didn't know him, but he was dressed like a Grogan Lubb. His legs were crushed and mangled, twisted in angles bones shouldn't go, and blood was all over. He looked more fucked-up than anyone I'd seen before, including guys we'd killed. Cops were watching, talking, but doing nothing.

"Where's the ambulance!?" Sammy shouted.

"Get back over by the wall!"

We backed off and waited again, but we'd discovered we had some freedom of movement, so after a few minutes I snuck up the alley to check on Amazin' and the others.

When I got back there I saw Solid and Ace—how'd he get there?—carrying Amazin' as best they could through the really narrow passage towards the grocery on Pearl. Toothless was on the other side of the fence waiting to help get him over.

"What up?" I asked as I went down to help.

"Ace says there's ambulances up on Silver and Fitzsimmons, but the cops won't let them come through."

"They been sitting up there for thirty minutes, but a cop got shot, so..."

"How you found us?"

"Toothless snuck out and came looking for help. We got a car over on Fitzsimmons. Let's see how far that takes us."

I helped hand Amazin' over the fence so Solid and the others could run him out to the waiting car, and when I saw they got off safe, I went back through the alleys to join the boys who were waiting, to fill them in on the situation.

"Cloud, we can get you out the other end of the alley. They say there's an ambulance up on Fitzsimmons."

"Well, what the fuck. Hold on a minute."

He led us out towards the street where the cops were.

"When are we going to get some help? You going to leave us out here to bleed, or what?"

"We already called ten times; the ambulance is coming, but you're not the only medical emergency."

"Who's in that car?"

"Back up."

"We don't got any weapons, you know that, we just want to see who's shot."

Cops were photographing the inside of the Nova. We pushed forward to see.

"Alright," one cop commanded, "clear them the fuck out of here."

"You mean we can go?" Sammy demanded.

"Just don't interfere here."

I got closer while the others were engaged.

"Fuck, they dead!" I said when I saw well enough to see Young—who was slumped in the passenger seat—and whoever it was that had his bloodied head pressed up on the steering wheel. It's creepy how you can instantly know the dead from the living. I couldn't recognize the driver, but it was Mesmer's car, so...

Cops pushed us back, and we almost stepped on the smashed up Grogan in the street.

Then Jonas said to me and Sammy, "We're taking him."

"Cool," said Sammy.

We bent and picked up the kid while his tortured shouts got more intense and his neck stiffened. Immediately a cop grabbed me to pull me off...

"Hey, what!..."

But Sammy and Jonas had the kid up, and they went running up the street with him towards where cops had the street blockaded with they cars.

"Stop! Stop!" the police shouted.

"We ain't letting you bleed this kid to death!" Jonas shouted back.

Cops in front of and behind them got they guns out, and one over by the blockade shouted, "Drop to the ground and don't move!!!"

Jonas and Sammy complied; they knelt down and lowered the wounded Grogan to the street again, but Jonas kept shouting:

"You going to kill him if you don't do something about

it now!"

When they were laid out prone again, cops rushed out... they'd already got me down, but I looked along the long, dark, black pavement into the lights and silhouettes as the cops rushed and cuffed Jonas and Sammy too...

"You better fucking get that ambulance here soon!" cried Sammy.

Cops were on they radios calling more urgently for back-up now, and I heard one of them demanding loud and clear, "Let's get that ambulance."

It wasn't but three more minutes until the ambulance arrived now, and they took that bleeding kid to safety. Sammy and I went to jail, while they took Jonas in cuffs to the hospital to check out his head-wound.

In jail, the holding cells were crowded because they were sweeping up pretty much everybody. They couldn't properly segregate us either. I hadn't even seen how Terrible got taken down in our struggle, but he wound up in the same holding cell with me and Sammy, eight other unknown guys, and one Grogan Lubb.

We were looking for a chance where we weren't getting watched so close, so we could fuck that guy up good and prop-er, but while guards were shuttling up and down the corridor, he started shit, knowing his beatdown would be interrupted quick, and that's exactly how it fell out. I squared the fucker, and Sammy and Terrible joined in, and we were sweeping the floor with him, but the guards got the cell open, got all the uninvolved parties laid out, and started beating on us and prying us off. Next, we got shifted to our own cell, and dude disappeared somewhere in the system.

Word came around quick Mesmer and Young were confirmed dead. Amazin' was in intensive care, and it wasn't certain he'd live.

Lettuce saw us briefly on our second day in, but besides commiserating over Mesmer and Young, he didn't have much to say because the authorities weren't answering any of his questions, and our usual lawyer was unavailable. Jonas visited us on day four. He'd been out the hospital after the first night. He had a big-ass bandage around his head, and he wore a cap to look more "normal."

"That wheezy guy, Sam," he said, "that came running up the alley? He backing us up, so the cops let me go. They would've let you go too, but now they want to hold you for assault."

"What assault?"

"In here."

"Oh, come on! They made that shit happen!"

"Just be patient. There'll be a bail hearing, and then Lettuce's got you."

"So, what else?"

"Everything man, shit is getting crazy. My house got burned."

"What!?"

"Probably white humans did that shit. They having parades out here, shouting 'Go back to Africa.' But it could've been the Grogans."

"Fuck, man, what's going on?"

"You would not believe it. Luckily, Lettuce has the treasury in a secure spot, and I got insurance, so we don't lose anything. But one girl, you know Steph?"

"Yeah, I know Steph."

"She was at my house, and she got shot in the face; the bullet came through the door."

"Oh no, she was pretty!"

"Yeah, she got knocked out. It kind of ripped her face and

smashed one cheekbone, but someone got her out before she burned, and she alright now. I saw her in the hospital."

"Fuck, man. What is wrong with humans?"

"Seriously."

"She's kind of like you, Cloud," said Terrible. "One or two inches this side of death."

"Yeah, or one or two inches this side of getting missed completely. Why you always gotta be so negative!"

"Heh."

"And we out here fighting every day. Every day. There's been no more shootings since day one, and Grogans mostly in hiding now, more scared of the whites than of us. But it's getting fistic in the streets, and we don't know when the fuck shit's going to get out of hand."

The next day there was a bail hearing. Lettuce had arranged a new lawyer to attend court. The initial charges of interfering with the law and disorderly conduct had been dropped. Though we were charged with assault, there had been no interview, so the only evidence was a written C.O.s report. We were released without bail, and Lettuce congratulated us on the way out the court.

"You are liberator!" shouted Sammy.

But shit was just getting worse out there. We were greeted on the outside with total lawlessness.

Let me tell you my own fucking opinion of rioting, because most humans got it all backwards:

A lot of humans get scared when they think of black men; they think of looting, mayhem, out of control violence. Now, it don't exactly profit our race to be seen stealing big-screen TVs and gold jewelry after a shooting, a hurricane, or a police assault. But let's be clear about what the fuck is going on. First of all, whites don't get to see the struggle of black humans until there's a riot. That's like a double whammy, first because it gives a false perception. Rioting isn't a normal black activity. Working your ass off for little pay and no respect is a normal black activity. Doing exactly what the white man says the black man is supposed to do to get ahead is a normal black activity, but it somehow winds up with the black man still at the bottom. But this is all invisible. So, riots just aren't the honest truth about black experience. They're just the visible sign of our plight.

But the other side of it is blacks get a message when they riots get broadcasted. *No one's going to pay attention unless you smash shit up. No one's going to hear you or take you serious until there's a crisis.* So of course there's riots, it's what whites watch TV for, it's what pays for the beer commercials and the tampon advertisements. Besides which, who the fuck convinced black kids a big-screen TV or gold chain is so desirable anyway? Consumerist America told us getting ahead is having these bullshit luxuries and escapist fantasies, so we're taking that shit.

The real distortion is that rioting is associated with black humans at all, when white riots are so much more destructive, sadistic, and common. Historically, it don't take much more than one black guy being a little disrespectful to a white lady before thousands of white maniacs come running in, burning orphanages, raping black women and cutting off black balls. That's no exaggeration. That's the shit really happens, historically, and not every riot or lynching makes the history books.

Some don't even make the daily papers. Seriously, white humans will riot if they team wins a hockey game. And humans riot everywhere in this world, all races. But the perception is blacks are the ones who are just unreasonable and make all kinds of crazy trouble. The reason humans get scared is because, on some gut level, they realize we Afros are sitting on some real potent rage that *hasn't been expressed yet.*

This time it started with some racist white parades, stirred up by the families of white waitresses got injured in the down-town bombing, and by supporters of the police who put the blame on us for every fucking thing. Then black humans lost they shit, and we had two more days of craziness to deal with. Whenever it was opportune during the conflict, if we ran up against one another, S·M·F battled Grogans. Eventually everyone was wore out, and humans who weren't from the neighborhood left us locals to deal with the fallout and continue our own scrapping on our own time.

When the warring calmed down, the overall toll was:

+ Two dead boys on our side from the first night, Young and Mesmer.

+ Three S·M·F gunshot wound survivors, including Amazin', who pulled through, Jonas with his head and ear wound, and Jelly, hit in the thigh.

+ One bullet-wounded police-officer, recovered.

+ Three Grogans with gunshot wounds, inflicted by police, all recovered.

- Minor-to-major injuries on all sides, ranging from
  sprained wrists to perforated liver:
  - About one third of our boys.
  - Maybe twenty-five Grogans.
  - Maybe a few cops with bruises.

- Felony charges with eventual convictions:
  - Five on Grogans,
  - None on us.

- Misdemeanors: Many.

- Civilian casualties: Who the hell knows?

- John Tarver, the leg-crushed Grogan who we saved,
  also had a fractured pelvis and spinal injury and never
  walked again (and went to prison). He owed his life to us,
  and he knew it.

That last circumstance, plus universal battle-exhaustion,
was the real first step towards peace, but hostile attitude and
suspicion remained.

Finally, news reached us about the downtown-poolhall
bomber, a guy named Irving Jamison. A Jack-Rabbit Lubb. He
got recognized from the sketches, and when he was arrested,
he snitched; he said Nolan Eason put him up to the bombing.
It was an attempt at revenge for Rashed Macklin, Nolan's ace
boon coon who got killed by the Grogans two years prior.

And what did this have to do with us? Nothing.

Wrong place, wrong time. Just sitting on a firecracker.

And with all this... with all this nonsense going on, in the
middle of everything... two eleven-year-old boys, unaffiliated
with any of us, were found hanged by the neck at the end of

the pier at *our* beach. Who did that shit, and why? It was an injury, not just to our city, but to our entire race. There was a police investigation, but they just called it "a mystery." We had to try to work it out ourselves on the street later, when some Walden Street Boys opened they mouths and claimed credit for the kill.

29.

A MONTH AND A HALF after the big fight, the Grogans were in a shambles. O.G. Wally Jackson reached out for a parley. Calvin Trice was out of the picture, supposedly retired, and now Jackson was the functional chief.

Jonas and I met him with his partners, and we brought Sammy along. Sammy was on a "situation-serious" warning, meaning he wasn't to fuck around in his usual way, but his purpose was to keep us straight and ensure we wouldn't make any unreasonable compromises.

When he met us, Jackson said, "We appreciate what you did for our boy..."

"Tarver?"

"Yeah. You got the kind of honor... humans just don't see that anymore, you know? We respect that."

"So what?"

"So, I'm just saying things fell out in a bad way. We appreciate you and the way you handled things. Even though a lot of our boys got hurt, and we going through a lot of shit right now..."

"You killed two of us."

"Yeah. Yeah, we did that."

"So what the fuck. I don't want to hear about respect. I ain't playacting here, you know? Put 'respect' on my tombstone."

Sammy said, "Our generol would like to know what you have in mind."

Jackson said, "We want to compensate you for your losses and make a resolution. We in a fiasco, and we gotta work things out."

"There's not going to be any *financial* resolution. You pay blood for blood."

"I've buried some of my own boys from time to time..."

"Fuck that."

"War has a heavy price, always, and peace never rolls back the clock. It just stops the loss. That's the best a reasonable man can hope for."

"Where's Calvin Trice?"

"He's done with. This shit didn't originate with me or anyone at this table."

"I heard he retired. What does that mean? Is he dead?"

"Our internal discipline is none of your concern."

"I heard he retired. What, with a comfortable pension? Where is he? He the fucker I should be negotiating with."

"That's not going to happen. And not like I didn't expect some steam. Fuck. We gotta work shit out, is all."

"I'll tell you how to start the negotiation," said Jonas. "You put Calvin Trice's head on the table. Then we start to talk."

"I... Listen. You bring tears to the table, we bring the gats. Who's going to get they way out of that?"

"You put his fucking head on the table," Jonas continued, undaunted, "so we can wash in his blood. Then you can start to tell us how we owe you peace."

We walked out.

We had met in a café at the top floor of a classy downtown hotel where an act of violence was sure to be observed. So the conflict, for now, was just words. In the elevator down, Jonas slapped Sammy on the shoulder with a loud clap.

"You did good Sammy. You did your job."

As for me, I hadn't spoken the whole time.

30.

WALDEN STREET is a street in many sections. You could even say there are several Walden Streets. But there's just a two-block section really matters in our history, the part that runs—west-to-east—from Belle Isle Street, to Nettleton Street, to Ridge Avenue. These are long, residential blocks, so two blocks would comprise maybe 150 houses plus some abandoned industrial spaces and empty lots—maybe 900 humans altogether. If you add in the two parallel streets north and south of Walden that fell within they province—that's Rose Street and Osbourne Street—then you got a small rectangular area most of us knew little about, with about 2,500 humans, many white, poor, and easily ignored. There was other races, but whites were a majority.

This little island was largely isolated from the not-quite-so-downtrodden, working-class, South-of-Yost whites. The area was bordered on three sides by majority black and Latino neighborhoods, with surrounding counts falling under Los Asesinos, S·M·F, and Carthage-Street Family-of-Man control. East of Ridge Avenue was concrete lots, desolated commercial properties, a couple of dollar stores. The area out there was unaffiliated, a no-man's land. La Fuerza Latina ran out there more often than anyone else, but that didn't mean anything. Mostly, there wasn't anything fun or even worthy to lay eyes on.

Fact was we didn't particularly hassle or associate with anyone in the Walden Street area. They lived they life, we lived ours. But, doubtless, some individuals had to experience some friction in they daily interactions. I would imagine they also had they domestic disputes and drunken squabbles just about as much as the rest of us.

From out this neighborhood came the two young boys who got hanged, David Serrant and Carlos Woods. Rumors had it they were killed for nothing more than mouthing off. I.e.

nothing. The rage that was felt by every member of the black community and every gangster of any persuasion was palpable. To kill two kids—not for revenge, not to enforce a law, not for anything but as a show of brutality—that couldn't stand. And the racial nature of the crime made it a real atrocity.

Walden Street Boys were just getting organized as a set, as a bunch of punk-ass whites trying to represent strength, doing it mainly by raising mayhem and committing petty robberies in they own community. Bottom-feeders.

As Sammy said, "White punks so skittish, if a deaf girl walked in they count talking sign language, they'd think she's set-tripping and break out running."

Piece by piece, we put together a story about the rise of they "lord," Jimmy Pricer—a hazy picture based on what *this* guy said and what *that* guy said...

Jimmy Pricer wasn't a native. He came to town just a few years back, and only sometimes stayed with his aunt on Walden Street, but he quickly whipped together a crew built up from locals were impressed by stories about killings he done.

He mainly built his reputation on shooting an old roommate named Covington he lived with in New Mexico. His excuse was some jealousy thing, and disrespect. He decided to shut up this boy's talk by challenging him to a shootout, and he offered to let him take the first shot—if you'll buy it. Pricer said Covington shot and missed, then he shot back and got him clean in the eye—through to the brain. He carried a clipping of a news article to support his story. We never got our hands on that article. Like I said, hazy.

Not everyone believed every detail of the stories he told, but when Serrant and Woods got hanged, doubts about Pricer's tales of murder were silenced. He went on to solidify his control of the count, and his boys became fanatical.

Despite our anger about what had happened, though, it was hard to motivate to do something. And it didn't look like no one else was going to do anything either. We were still civil with Los Asesinos, but we weren't exactly strongly tied, and the word filtered out they would only get involved if Walden Street Boys crossed over into they count, or if one of the known captains made hisself a conspicuous target. Carthage Street Lubbs had the strongest motive to move on Walden Street, but they were reputationally weak. They aimed to keep they small-scale dope-pushing going without rousing any attention from authorities, and I think they prayed every night no one would fuck with them. As for us... we had to constantly watch our backs with the Grogans, we had to rebuild our strength, we had legal problems all over, with some boys still down for misdemeanor assaults and such, and just getting business back to some state of normalcy was a struggle.

But I'm not exactly telling the whole truth with regards to the "word" on the street. "Word" had it every motherfucker was ready to rush in, rip those Walden Street Boys to shreds, tear the fucking captains apart with they moms watching, and no one feared any reprisals, they'd run through storms of gunfire to get to those punks... You get the picture. But "word" did not initially turn into action, except there was one unfortunate circumstance.

Carthage Street caught some white middle-school kids walking on Yost. One of them was said to be the younger brother of a Walden Street Boy. They shot them up. Two kids were wounded, and the whole white community, both in Walden Street, and in the "better" parts of town, rose up in indignation. Walden Street Boys' recruitment went up; they might have doubled they strength in response to that irresponsible shooting, and afterwards white kids were sometimes accompanied in they walks along Yost—even on Carthage Street itself—by groups of ten or twenty self-appointed "defenders," claiming the only purpose they served was to make they neighborhood secure.

Adults got posted in "neighborhood watch" patrols at night.

And a while after that, the "Lord of Walden Street," Jimmy Pricer, came out and marched in midday with about fifty of his boys to rally in Brandywine Park. No more than a couple of our boys were nearby to see it, and some reporters came out. When I was told what was going on, I moved quick to the park with six soldiers. There was lots of witnesses all around.

"No one in our neighborhood," said Pricer, "had anything to do with the tragic deaths of either David Serrant or Carlos Woods. We will not be scapegoats. The boys who spread that rumor were just trying to get the message out we can't be trifled with. But it was a mistake to even encourage humans to think we could do, or would approve of such a thing."

"Not true!" shouted a young black man of maybe eighteen, nineteen. "You lying! I heard you come walking around saying niggers is going to die if they don't respect Walden Street Boys! How you think you can say something like that?!"

"When someone gets hurt, the community gets angry. But rumors are attaching to us unfairly. We *only* want to live in peace and security in our own homes and on our own streets."

"I seen you with my own face, and my cousin got beat up..."

"Walden Street is the neighborhood where me and my friends live," Pricer continued. "We call it home, and we do not have to tolerate being intimidated."

"Who intimidating you? You boys said 'Don't mess around or we hang you like we did them other two.' Word to God, you said that."

At this point we'd pushed our way through the crowd and started fighting the Walden Street Boys and they defenders. Other bystanders also got involved. Walden Street Boys didn't employ any weapons except for whatever came to hand—one swung a bicycle chain—and we fought unarmed except for sticks and bottles. The scrap went on for maybe twenty minutes, but the Walden Street Boys managed a retreat. They got they leader out safely, and most of us had to dodge to avoid getting nabbed when the cops started breaking it up.

31.

A DIALOG between two S·M·F soldiers—unnamed—that typifies the mood of the time:

"Don't believe that shit about they didn't do nothing. They can't have it both ways. First they want to say they hanged those kids so humans gotta fear them, but then they say no, it's just a rumor. That's bullshit. There's some things you don't lie on yourself about. Would you go out and try to build a reputation on being a child molester or something like that?"

"No."

"You know what I'm talking about. They manipulating sympathies, but we the ones been out here from the beginning fighting only for what's right…"

"Sure, sure…"

"And now this fucking scrub Pricer comes out talking about he some kind of hero to the white community—like white humans need *another* hero, right?"

"But still, how do we know?"

"Fuck what we know, brother. We gotta prove it in a court of law? Just saying they did it…"

"We only heard *someone else* say they said they did it."

"It don't matter. Today you could show humans absolute proof. You could put the crime right before they eyes, and still they say '*How we know?*' They skeptical. But reputation and image count for something, and we know that motherfucker a racist bastard, and it's time to put an end to that shit. I think sometimes I know more about *you* than you know yourself…"

"Fuck that."

"It's true. I do. I know more about him… and him… I know about a lot of humans because I'm wise and observant, and I'm not the skeptical kind says '*How we know?*' to everything. Sometimes we gotta trust our instincts on what's obvious."

"Maybe what's obvious to them is we out here robbing

cars and shit, and we got knives, and we be killing humans, and they scared."

"*Are you fucking going to defend those murdering cocksuckers!!!?*"

"No, I'm not saying that..."

"Goddamn! When they murder the innocent. Children, man, come on..."

"I'm not defending anyone, I'm just saying, if you going to go by what's 'obvious'..."

"We're not having this conversation."

32.

WE HAD ONE GO at trying to kill Jimmy Pricer. A big rock show was taking place at the Clifford Arena downtown. Three big-name bands were playing as part of a national tour. Sammy answered the phone when we were hanging at Jonas's place.

"What...? Yeah, cool, where...?"

You got it. Sammy gave us the gist of the conversation.

"Quite-Right said there's white kids all over and they buying weed and acid out this van two blocks from the show. It's Walden Street Boys..."

We were in our cars on our way to the show when Sammy explained to Jonas how they knew, and who recognized who... I was driving my own car so I missed that part of the discussion. I stopped when I saw Jonas stop, maybe a quarter mile from the arena, because the traffic was out of hand. I had to park partway in a pedestrian crossing, pretty conspicuously. We got out and rallied, then went on foot.

"We just gotta go, and if we lucky we disperse in the crowd."

"What does Pricer drive?"

"Drive? He gets drove. Thinks he a star. Quite-Right says his car and driver are caddy-corner to the van where his boys are. It's a black Continental. Tanya told him she recognized Pricer getting in and out the car twice, going to a convenience store once, and checking on his boys."

It was a hike, and when we got there we were too late. Barely.

Quite-Right was getting dragged out the back seat of the Lincoln by two guys, while on the other side of the car, in the street, Pricer got picked up off the pavement and pushed back in the car by a guy who was helping him. We ran up, and the car pulled out and drove past us before we could do anything. Pricer's face was bloody.

Tanya, Quite-Right's snaggle-toothed ho, was standing around crying uselessly.

"What happened!?"

We got Quite-Right up and running and made our escape with Tanya trailing along.

"The driver started the car, so I thought I just had to act. No time…" Breathlessly telling his story. "There was a guy already in the car between me and him. I got my blade on him… They were all over me, you know, and Pricer was already out the car…"

Back on secure ground, we applauded Quite-Right's initiative, but it hadn't really paid off. Then our minds were on other things.

33.

Business was *starting* to normalize, at the same time discipline was getting a little shoddy. Rollup, Cookie, and No-Love found they way out the click, but twenty-two of our thirty-two founding members were still together through the years. Some younger soldiers had come and gone, but our overall numbers swelled with additional recruits drawn in from loyal babies, new arrivals to the neighborhood, and additional motherfuckers from our expanded count.

Horseback was a captain again, and, after a reorganization, his team was made up of mostly younger brothers. One day I heard him schooling a baby on the lit.

"Who smashed the ox-cart of freedom?" Horseback asked.

"Frederick Douglass," said the baby.

"What!?" I shouted.

I quickly brought my fist down on the skull of his bitch-head.

"What you say?"

The wannabe answered me from where he lay on the concrete, holding his neck. I'd accidentally hurt him more seriously than I'd intended. "Frederick Douglass."

"But did you listen to the question?"

He seemed confused and defensive. "That's how I learned it."

"Come with me Jeff."

I drew Horseback aside about a dozen steps, but some boys were lingering about, listening.

"Did you ask him the wrong question intentionally?"

"No."

"Don't teach the lit if you don't know it!" I shouted. "It's the ox-cart of slavery, you fuck! Do you think freedom has the same meaning as slavery?"

He blinked at me.

"I don't know. That's how we been teaching it."

"You getting violated!"

I thought he would make a contest of it, but Horseback just said, "I'm sorry Mala. I was wrong."

I was going to hit him... I drew back my fist... but then I placed my hand on his cheek in the token of a slap. I couldn't deliver the blow. It was a shameful moment for me.

What had I taught all them anyhow? Nothing but some names, arbitrary facts, and cryptic riddles without a moral, because in my still-youthful vanity I couldn't admit I was no more educated than the rest of them.

34.

SHORTLY AFTER THAT, Market got released on an early parole. That surprised us. But he didn't come around.

Thayne and I went out to see him when we heard where he was staying downtown. He was crashing for a while with an old motherfucker with braided hair stinking of weed.

"What up!?"

We gave Market his hugs, but then he shut us down quick.

"I gotta tell you boys, I'm sorry, but I'm out."

"What you mean, *out?*"

"Fuck that, what? Brothers for life."

"I'm telling you, I'm cool with you two, but I got nothing to do with S·M·F. I'm done."

"What the fuck, man. No."

"I'm in with the Ancient Order now."

He turned to a piece of dirt right in front of our eyes. I was knocked out.

"You couldn't tell us that when you was down!?" Thayne shouted. "Come on, how long you been sitting on this?"

"When was the last time you saw me?"

"We been communicating with you," I told him. "You had a thousand chances to tell us what was up. You need help, you tell us."

"I gotta look out for me. Listen. They don't know shit from S·M·F inside, and that's a fact. It's a survival thing. They took me in, man, and it's lucky too."

"No, fuck that. Efrem's loyal and always will be. He's facing harder time than you. Nap and Heaven too."

"Whatever goes on with them, that's they own business, but I'm telling you. I'm out."

Thayne got mad. "You going to stand here in my face and tell me that shit? You don't know that's fucking a capital offence? You could have negotiated with us or something. Now you put yourself in a dangerous position."

"I'm doing you a favor and telling you now rather than try to scheme an out. I know… Look, I'm moving to California, so you don't have to worry about me fucking up your shit."

"I'm telling you, you a fucking punk."

"There's no beef between us. A.O. is a lifesaver to me, and they got all my heart. You all, no offence, you're a part of my long-gone past."

"In a thousand years I wouldn't have turned against the S·M·F. In a thousand years. You fucking rat."

"Just let it go, okay? You're not that mad, I know it. And I'm not going to spend my life as a sucker on a principle. What you got to say, Mala?"

"I got nothing to say. You turned is all."

"No, you got something more than that to say," said Thayne. "Tell him."

"Yeah, well, he's not us. He buckled. Fuck him."

The old ratty dude Market was living with looked like he wanted to say something on our way out, but he kept his mouth shut. Wisely so.

Outside, Thayne stopped me before we could go far.

"Hold up. This ain't right," he said. "We letting too many fuckers get away with too much shit."

"Yeah, I know what you mean, but…"

"Taboos are taboos for a reason. Think about it Mala."

"I know, serious. Ah, fuck. You right." I paused to think a moment. But I knew I couldn't let a doubt creep in. "Alright. Alright, let's… ah, let's do business."

We walked back in. No one had moved yet to lock the door. We got our blades out and started cutting without another thought. Market fought hard, and he was still fighting when we'd put five or six deep wounds in his chest, belly, and thigh, plus slashed up his arms and hands. The other guy struggled to pull us off and landed a couple of punches on the back of my head, and I cut his cheek, but he wasn't putting up a full-hearted fight of it because our attention wasn't on him so much and he wasn't committed to die... like, he wasn't going to grapple or let anything come between him and the exit-door in case he had to bolt. And in fact, when Thayne turned on him, he did just that, but he called from just outside: "That's enough. You don't gotta kill him!"

I agreed. I tugged Thayne's shoulder while Market was kind of crab walking back across the floor and kicking out his foot.

"Yeah, let's go," I said.

"*This* was going easy, bitch," said Thayne to Market. "You better dream of me coming for you every night, and wake up thankful if it's only a dream."

As we came out, the A.O.-bum kept a safe distance and let us pass.

Word filtered back to us eventually that Market survived and moved to California as he planned.

35.

HELL IS UNDERSTANDABLE. Heaven is understandable. But earth is not a place that can be comprehended.

Being imprisoned, being persecuted unjustly, being tortured, living "free" in a world that will gladly watch you starve, not knowing when someone's going to come along and try to cut your balls off... getting insulted and blamed daily, being told you're the problem and the extermination of your kind is the solution—this is normal. This is the normal state of affairs for human beings. It's a blessed state not to know this, but it's more honest to open your eyes and face it.

Look. What you think happens when all this shit is over, huh? For you or for me. You think we headed for a happy end where all our problems wash away—where we can say "I'm proud to have reached this point in my life?" The only humans I ever heard speak that way were out of they minds; they chanted that shit like it was a magic spell.

The magic didn't work.

I spoke to one punk robber one time, a guy we couldn't take in the click because his past was so nasty. Fucker robbed old ladies; fucker got blind drunk and beat on his friends; fucker one time jerked hisself off on a bus full of humans and laughed about it. When I asked him about his funky ways, he set out to rationalize hisself. He said to me, "If I rob you, or beat you, or victimize you in some way, I know it hurts. I'm sorry for it, sometimes. But at the same time, I'm doing you a favor. I'm waking you up. I'm educating you to the truth. If you piss your pants, and you have nightmares from now on, and you feel hate for me and humans like me... congratulations, you've learned. Terror is the natural state of affairs, you ought to feel it. You're on the edge all the time, all the time; I ain't lying." And you know what? He was right in every fucking word.

And we S·M·F, with our moral codes, we tried to hold ourselves somehow above that, but to tell the truth, he knew something.

And I'm telling you, for God's sake, don't you ever put me in a position where I call all the shots, where my power is unlimited. I promise you, if the circumstances were right, and I was the authority, the street lamps would be festooned with human skin. Life is pain down in the marrow of your bones, and I can deliver that shit just as well as I can receive it.

Jonas saved me every day, but sometimes I wasn't thankful at all. I was angry. I wanted to ram his head right up a cow's ass, right into the shit. I would have put a bullet in my skull if I could, but he kept that tool out of my hands, and alcohol couldn't take me away from myself when I felt the rages sweating me right through the clothes. I'd have swallowed my own head if I could have got my gums around it.

Where's our gas chamber, humans? This is no fucking joke! Society, get your act together and gas us all.

36.

WE HAD ANOTHER O.G. meeting and talked about the practicalities. I had been thinking about things and had a proposal.

"What's going on with the money?" I asked.

"What you mean?"

"I mean... Lettuce, you said we made two-point-two million dollars on loans this past year."

"Yeah."

"But you didn't say how much from car robbing."

"We weren't talking about that, but that comes to about... one-point-four, about."

"Alright, and gambling?"

"Looks like less than a quarter million dollars, or... in that range. Burglaries and other business, maybe a hundred twenty thousand more."

"Well I'm going to suggest something, and I know it sounds crazy. But I say we need to stop robbing cars entirely."

"Yeah, that's radical," said President with a laugh.

"Why?" asked Jonas.

"We can sustain ourselves off the lending. It's just about risk. I mean, we ain't never got busted on any serious charges related to lending."

"Yeah, but you're talking about serious revenue!"

"It don't matter. We coming to a turning point. Plus, after we lost Efrem and his garage, the new garage don't pay so well and we don't really know who we dealing with. And we don't need complication right now with pressure all over the place."

"But you know just a couple million dollars don't go so far with expenses. We got boys going in and out the hospital, we got legal costs and payments to bail-bondsmen. We got something close to fifty mouths to feed too..."

"Forty-seven."

"...plus entertainment."

"Plus," said Lettuce, "we got an increasing need to keep cash."

"Look, radical solutions need to be given serious consideration. It's just dumb putting our boys in risk all the time when we can take care of them, and our neighborhood, in better ways. Plus, most of our legal expenses you talked about come directly from robbing, so you can't just charge that to the account of all S·M·F business. It overrates robbing and underrates the profit of lending."

Jonas said, "You're not thinking. The real issue is most of the boys, especially the newer ones, don't have any other way to contribute. We can't all be lenders and collectors. And some are just... they need an outlet, you know. We getting old, but they young."

"I *am* thinking," I countered, "and I know where you coming from, but it don't have to be this way. And we can stop other burglaries altogether, unless someone concocts a seriously big heist at low-risk, which is unlikely."

"Okay, that's something we can think about."

"As for the rest, we can reintroduce the young ones into gambling-related operations and expand there. Prez, you gotta be down with that."

"Nah, I still have to care about the bottom line, however we earn it."

"Yeah, listen," said Lettuce, "if we put more kids into gambling, fact is most of them will collect more in shares than they contribute."

"So what?"

"Come on! Get real," said President.

"No, I am real," I said. "I'm saying... we deserve a peace dividend when times are peaceful. Kids has earned they stripes. And when times are *not* peaceful, they still face risk as soldiers any time they get called on. It's fair enough to compensate for that. We just gotta stop expanding our ranks; we don't need so many kids at the soldier level no more."

"Ah... Seriously, seriously," said Thayne. "You got a noble heart, but I don't see that makes any business sense."

"Jonas, I'm talking to you personally now..."

"Nah, shut up," said President. "Don't play manipulation games."

"This is no game. I'm for real. If I'm wrong, I'm wrong. But fact is, we in this for the good of our click, for our soldiers, and, Hell... even if they don't know what's best for them, we're experienced to know what's better. We can help them out, and honor ourselves for that."

Jonas said, "I respect your point of view. We're going to think about it. Maybe not a 180 degree flip, just a change. We can do with a reminder once in a while of what we in the game for. Thanks."

But the result of this conversation was minimal. We trained up some younger soldiers to help run the gambling business. We got our numbers games into two more Silver Avenue bodegas where we hadn't done business before. We even put together a team of five older players, headed by Fierce, who'd been gambling for years and showed some really excellent poker skills. We sent them out to try to hustle dollars in some California card-rooms, with a little stopover in Vegas on the way. I wish I'd gone with them. But after all, they only cleared maybe $12,000 in three months over expenses (but I bet they ate well!), so we called them home.

In time we saw about a 40% increase in gambling revenue, and a 9% decrease in car robbing, for a small overall loss of profit, but kids were getting into just about as much trouble. One got busted for possession of a stolen vehicle, two for having burglary tools, and one of the newer kids, a guy named Jody "Swift" Washington, got his head cracked by a big and angry owner.

Jonas wanted to do what's right, but it wasn't easy to reform our ways.

37.

"So, I GOTTA TELL YOU about a call I got," said Jonas.

"Who from?" I asked.

We were having a private discussion over at Uncle James's bar again while watching a fight on TV.

"Let me tell you the story. I was just relaxing, you know, on Thursday. The phone rings. I pick it up and it's someone I don't recognize. 'Hi. I want to place a bet,' he says. Well, I said, 'This is not a work number' and hung up, but he called right back. So then he says 'I want to put $50,000 on Glen Fields in his Saturday fight against Funches.'"

"That fight's on right now!"

"I know. So I ask him, 'You know the odds?' 'No' he says. So I tell him 'You picked a dog. You get 220. That's 11 to 5.' 'Cool,' he says, 'I'll send a representative over with the money post-haste.' 'Who is this?' I ask him..."

"And?"

"He says 'This is Calvin Trice.'"

"You're kidding."

"Not kidding."

"What the fuck does *he* want?"

"Well, he tells me all sorts of shit. He angry. There's a schism in the set. He wants to know when we going to come out of mourning and take the war back to the Grogans. I ask him, 'What's going on over there?' and he goes off about how disloyalty is the one thing he can't stand, and he talking about all kinds of shit I don't understand about the other Lubbs and how they disowned him. He wants to cut a deal with us where we help him, and he helps us to take the Grogans apart. He even says to me, 'I can give you all the heads you want to make a settlement. You just gotta come and retrieve them.'"

"So... someone's talking to him."

"Gotta be. I don't know, he could still be in with the Grogans, playing some kind of game or something. But he says he wants Wally Jackson dead."

"What happened next?"

"Well, we didn't settle anything else but the bet. He sent over a courier with the $50,000 cash."

"You took his bet?"

"Yeah... Uncle James, turn up the audio!"

Uncle James complied.

The fight had started off as an impressive contest. Both fighters had come out to fight, trading strong blows early, both showing commitment and landing a lot of straight punches with speed and accuracy. But in the third round, Fields was starting to get in trouble.

In an exchange in the middle of the ring, Funches found an opening, caught Fields with a powerful left hook, and followed with a combination that took him to the canvass. Fields was up within three seconds, his legs wobbly, when Funches immediately brought it to him with a new flurry of blows—it was looking like this might be it—but Fields withstood everything Funches could throw, and by the end of the round he had his feet back under him. He was punishing Funches back, showing he wouldn't die early. Both fighters were strong, and it was shaping up to be a great fight.

I wanted to talk to Jonas about what was going on with the Walden Street Boys. War had started in earnest between them and Carthage F.O.M., and boys on both sides were getting wounded. One Lubb died. But the fight on TV had taken on a new dramatic significance.

The fourth round was Funches's, just barely. Fields was continuing aggressively like he felt the fight was his, not desperate, but driven. Both fighters were showing a lot of heart, and they were both fast, getting in a lot of clean hits, almost all upstairs, with only the occasional body blow. Funches wasn't much for circling, and when he got backed up, he stepped right back in with jabs and counter-punches to keep Fields off, only to have Fields come right back at him. And when the bell rang, for me, the main impression was *Wow, Fields is still in it.*

In the fifth round, they boxed more, but it was still sharp, fast, and dramatic. They were strong on the attack, but they were also blocking well. Fields was bloody, but his head was in the game. When it was near the center of the ring they seemed evenly matched. Then Fields got Funches backed in a corner and punished him for a good fifteen, twenty seconds. Funches managed to back him off and work his way out again. After another twenty seconds back-and-forth, the bell rang. That was Fields's round.

Sixth round established a new pattern. Fields stayed on the aggressive with a lot of forward motion, both kept they guard up and exploited every opportunity, a few more body blows were landed, and Fields backed Funches into a corner twice, but each time Funches got cornered he immediately came out with power and backed Fields the fuck off. Even when he'd already been fighting a strong fight, he really came to life when coming out of the corner, and Fields had to stand up to a lot of damaging blows, sharp jabs, and more straight rights that found they target. Seventh round looked the same, with Funches playing very effective defense, fighting well out of the corner, ending a great combination with a solid right hook that hurt Fields, and getting in counter-blows in response to every good combination Fields delivered for the rest of the round.

The eighth round was decisive. Fields kept coming on regardless of Funches's strong counterplay. He went upstairs, then got in another good body blow. On the surface, both fighters seemed still in the fight; if anything, Fields looked to be getting hit harder in the first minute, but then he was getting in jab, and jab, and jab, and then a nice right. The accumulation of damage just told on Funches—he couldn't quite get hisself out of trouble and his countering was getting less effective.

Fields could keep coming, and he got another straight right that dazed Funches. There was little visible evidence, but the turning point had come. Funches backed up, as before, back to the corner, but there was no fighting his way out this time. A flurry of blows took his defense apart enough so Fields could hit him with a head-rocking left-uppercut; then more blows rained and jarred Funches so the ref had to stop it as he sank to his knees. There was no question this was a legit TKO.

Wow. Big fight.

The rest of the night was speculating about what we would say when we met Calvin Trice, but we didn't have much of a clue.

⨯

Trice met us in another bar. For shits we chose a place in the middle of what used to be Black Steel Nines territory, in the eastern Wild-Zone where it had been absorbed by Los Asesinos, just outside the Grogans' reach. We were inclined to show no regard for domain at the time. The choice of site was dangerous for Trice. For us it was maybe a little apolitical.

Trice delivered hisself right into our hands. We could have turned the meeting into a turkey-carving. But Jonas owed Trice $160,000, and psychologically he couldn't renege on a bet. And wouldn't it be a little silly to deliver payment into a guy's hands only to kill him in the next moment? But in all events, Trice was willing to meet us almost anywhere and trust in Jonas's sense of honor. That's how he played us.

At the first mention of money, Trice said, "Keep it. I was expecting to lose. You make that a part of the compensation for the boys you lost. I'm seriously sorry for that."

"We don't take cash payment."

"It don't matter, that's why I said *part*. You'll get all the real payback you want. Listen, Grogans is falling apart, as you know. And that's not my doing. They did it to theyselves..."

We let him go on.

"What you don't know, probably, is Wally Jackson is in so deep he don't know what to do. His betrayal of me has shook up the whole set to the point half the boys want out if they can find somewhere better to run to, and most of the rest would like for anything to see Wally crushed in his fucking arrogance. He's not a leader of my quality. And while I had no friends... fuck, that's crazy to say..."

"Come on, what's your point?"

"Seriously, dude, you don't know what it's like to have everything torn away from you when you worked so hard."

"I don't think you walked away empty handed."

"When it comes to money, I got that shit, yeah. I could retire to Barbados tomorrow. Maybe I will. But it's the fucking rats. I got a lot of love for my boys, and some of them got love for me back, except Wally exploited them in the moment when everyone was kind of shook up, you know, blaming each other, trying to see who can keep they neck loose from the noose, you know? Wally promised to get things straight and made me the whipping boy. Well fuck, I took a vacation that turned into exile. Only, Wally's stepped on too many toes. You know Simms?"

Jonas explained to me, "He was at the meeting we had. Dude next to Wally."

"No one introduced me," I said.

"Anyway," said Trice, "he's usually solid. It was a moment of weakness for him when he let Wally start calling the shots. But in his heart... Well, fuck his heart, I ain't going to lie. He says he's loyal to me, but I know he got his own ambition. Anyway, he's ready to try to pull a coup if I can support him."

"Yeah, yeah, okay, look," said Jonas. "You got a complicated situation. But what's stopping you from stepping in and just blasting shit up? I mean, we don't need you, and I don't see where you want to get us involved."

"Are you crazy? Come on. The Grogans gotta come apart, or they gotta come to me. But I can't draw blood on a brother nohow. I'll be persona non grata in every Family click world-wide. There won't be any comfort for me even in a jail cell. It got to come from outside, and you the boys who are expected to take the war back to them."

"We don't need your encouragement."

"But you could use my information. I got an in with Rudy Simms. He knows everything goes on. He's smarter than Wally Jackson, and he can lead Wally anywhere. He's a fucking Judas Iscariot for manipulation, I tell you."

I said, "How the fuck you wind up with humans like that for friends? And how are we supposed to work with you like that?"

"You don't know humans sometimes until they tested by adversity. And we never knew adversity until what we went through, first with Nines, then Jack-Rabbits, then with Eason, and finally with you motherfuckers. Said with respect."

"Do you know what happened to Nolan Eason?"

"No. Do you?"

"No."

"Well anyway, I'm telling you I can deliver Wally Jackson into your hands. I don't even care. Maybe there'll be no place for me after, but I don't give a fuck. We gotta deal with business one step at a time."

"I'm sorry," said Jonas, "but a little information isn't going to settle things with us."

"Fuck it, you can come for me after, but I'm still going to help you out. I can even arm you up."

"We don't need weapons."

"Maybe in this case you do. Maybe suspend your laws for a day. War plays by its own rules. But listen. I know you, Cloud. Jonas. I been studying you. I respect you deeply, more than you think. I got my practical side, I don't see eye-to-eye with you on everything. But I understand you a little, and it's nice you want to do good by humans. You gotta know I got my own laws too, and my morality. Wally's just overturned that; he's the devil in our set."

"You talk like the devil yourself."

"Heh, maybe."

"I don't want to play any games, though," said Jonas. "And I don't trust your proposition. Mala and I are going to have to talk and think about things for a while, but for now I have to say no go. You can take your money and go your way."

"No, no, I ain't taking no money. That bet was just a joke."

"There's no joking when it comes to bets and the S·M·F."

"Then call it a teaser. It was just a way to open up the conversation."

"Anyway…"

"And I'm telling you, it can be a real benefit having a tight ally. You know, no more pressure in your back, so you're free to pursue whatever your interests are. Just wait a while, you'll get another call from me."

"Number's changed."

"Then look for smoke signals. But I'm not desperate. Rudy Simms and I'll work things out our own way. I just thought you'd relish this opportunity to get some payback. And what's up with you, Mala?"

"What you mean?"

"You're supposed to be advising him, am I right? Try to talk him into being more Machiavellian, right? He should have tried to play me for a while instead of just shutting down the conversation at the start."

"Well, you know. Cloud is straight."

"And you're not going to contradict that, and neither am I. Well, that's cool. Have a good night, y'all."

He took his sack of cash. We wondered if some boys would come in soon to shoot us in our seats. But that didn't happen, and we went home in our own time.

38.

Jonas took us cruising in his recently acquired white Buick Riviera convertible with maple interior. Jonas and Amazin' were in the front seats, and it was me and Fierce in the back. The top was down; it was a nice ride. Night was upon us.

After surveying the scene in the usual spots, and after a detour downtown, Jonas turned us back and we rolled towards Walden Street. I'd never seen it before.

Things was *dark* and *quiet*. No one on the sidewalk. The breeze was in our face as we glided down the street.

"If the bullets fly, Fierce, you catch them," said Jonas.

"Why me?"

"Your turn."

I laughed, which triggered a rasping cough and a twinge of pain. Damn. I'd already been feeling mighty old after I witnessed Amazin's slow, awkward struggle climbing into the passenger seat, and now I sounded pathetic.

"You alright back there?" asked Jonas.

I thought it too shameful to reply.

"If there's a neighborhood watch, they watching through closed blinds," said Fierce.

"I'm telling you, it's like this," said Jonas.

"You know where Pricer lives?"

"No. And it don't matter because I hear he spends most of his time outside the count somewhere. Lets his soldiers handle strife, and he's never been seen in the front of any conflict."

"He acts like that and they still respect him?"

"White people crazy."

"Deluded."

Jonas slowed, then stopped out front of an abandoned house with black spray-paint on the steps and more paint on the boards that covered the door frame and front windows. There were some flowers on the stoop.

"God damn," said Jonas. "Some babies told me the spray-paint house is where the Serrant kid lived."

"Why they come and desecrate it?" said Amazin' and tsk-tsked.

"Friends painted an R.I.P. message, but the neighbors painted over it saying graffiti spoil the neighborhood. When kids come back to paint another message, the Walden Street Boys blot it out with they filthy black scrawls. The neighbors have given up trying to clean it."

"This is sick, man; I don't want to look at it."

"That's why you gotta fucking look at it."

We looked for another half a minute, then moved on.

We got over to Ridge Avenue and turned south. A police cruiser started following along behind us.

Two blocks on, as we were crossing the Ridge–Yost intersection, in the big vacant lot across the way we saw a group of about twenty, thirty Lubb-looking Afros making a conspicuous standing target of theyselves. The cop flashed his lights and pulled us over while the Carthaginians looked on in curiosity.

"License and registration."

"Yes, officer." Jonas leaned across and pointed as Amazin' opened the glove compartment. "That leather folder there."

Jonas handed the documents to the cop, who inspected them for a moment, then walked back to his car and kept us waiting.

"Cops all know who I am. They done checked twice to be sure this really my car. Like they can't believe it. But I thought they stopped hassling me lately."

"But we in a new jurisdiction now."

The cop came back and returned the documents, and shined his flashlight in, looking around.

"I'd like to check your car just to be sure everything's safe."

"I'm sorry officer, I don't consent to searches."

"I need to ask you to step out and let me be sure we don't have any problems."

"What's to see?" asked Fierce. "The top's down; you already seen everything."

"You got any weapons in the trunk, glove compartment, under the seats?"

"No, officer, and I don't consent to searches," said Jonas.

"Are you boys up to any trouble around here?"

"No."

"Listen. There's been gang violence out this way. Don't get mixed up in it, alright?"

"We won't."

"Alright, you go on your way then."

"Yes, sir."

We got moving again, and we turned off on Carthage. I looked back and saw the Lubbs watching us drive on they street. I saw the cherries on they bats glow in the darkness as they receded from our view.

"Listen," said Jonas, "that's basically how you handle a stop. We don't get out of hand."

"We all know that."

"They all know me, but so long as I don't give them any excuse, they been cutting me slack. Don't say shit to them like 'You already seen everything.'"

"That's true though."

"It don't matter what's true."

"Sorry, Cloud."

"You don't play smart, and you don't play dumb; you just play straight and cooperative."

Carthage Street was as quiet as Walden. The whole atmosphere was eerie. Well, not quite. There was two Lubbs smoking and drinking on one stoop we passed by. Besides that, the count could've been a graveyard.

The next part of our tour took us up Nettleton, which showed more of the same, until we crossed up through a section of Los Asesinos count. Kids were lively there, lights were on in houses, they were listening to that Salsa-Mariachi or whatever shit they listen to. But they were having fun, and why not. It was Friday night.

One group jumped up from they stoop and turned on us. They represented Asesinos, and one shouted out, "Don't get cocky, Cloud. This ain't your place to be!" But we passed on unmolested, and all was cool.

"It's nice to get recognized."

Across the ocean everything was lively too, even more so, and lots of kids were out having fun in little groups. We got more attention from spectators scoping, observing our ride.

We turned west on Carlo and started a tour of the Grogan count, and I thought, *Fuck, Jonas loses his mind sometimes.*

"I don't know about you and your thrill seeking aspect," I said. "Why we gotta come out here?"

"You want me to turn back?"

"Would you, if I told you to do it?"

"Yeah. I would."

"Nah, I'm not going to say no. But I wonder."

Businesses were open. Civilians were out. There was a sense of tension, I didn't hear any cheerful chat or laughter, and people walked kind of quiet. But people were out. The thing was, there was no visible Grogan presence anywhere. Anywhere. We saw what looked like one little deal going on in an alley between a black guy and a white tourist, but no one was representing the set.

"What the fuck?"

"They all scared of each other now," said Jonas.

"You knew it would be like this?" I asked.

"No. But I thought maybe. It's worse than I thought, actually, but think: Captains are forming they own little sub-clicks, plotting they own little dramas, looking over they shoulders all the time. Soldiers probably follow they leaders. They go downtown for fun, or they stick at home. They sell as much product as they have to while lurking in shadows, then get off the street. No one stands out waiting to get it from whatever sub-faction wants to act first. Business is business, but the bonds are broken. What you think, Blaise?"

"It's weird and ugly. You don't think they just scared of us, though?"

"There's that. But they spirit's crushed. If they so scared in they own count, you think they'll ever have the heart again to cross over into ours?"

We were riding down Fitzsimmons now, towards home.

I said, "If Trice were in command, I think they'd find the heart again."

"Maybe."

Back in the corner, life was cheery. It was odd how a little drive gave a new perspective on conditions in our own count. This little place that was once so dismal was now breathing free and easy since we liberated it. Not just gang-life, but civilian life was better. Families were up and around at night. Bodegas that we had financed with our loans were operating, and some neighbors made runs up to Silver to buy from the new Shazaam we had also financed. Young kids rode they bikes at 10:30 and they moms didn't call them back. Even in a few houses I saw some humans keep they inner doors open and catch a breeze through the screen door. I hadn't seen that even on Ducasse when I was a kid, and here it was where the Lubbs once ran.

"We living nice now," said Jonas. "And I think all the pressure we been feeling has been mostly illusion."

"That, and memory," I said.

Amazin' said, "But Young ain't here to feel this."

"I know," said Jonas. "I figured that's gotta upset you. But what you think, anyway?" After some silence, Jonas pulled the car over to a stop. Then he asked Amazin' again, "What do you think about the way things stand?"

"I want to burn the fucking Grogans, man. I want them to pay. We got ghosts calling out for vengeance."

Jonas turned, looked at me, and shook his head a little. Then he said to Amazin', "I think that feeling's always going to be with us. But we gotta take care of our living brothers."

"I'm not so happy with this fucking world."

"But we can't give it back to the one's we lost."

Amazin' got angry.

"Come on! If you can't satisfy the least of our grudges, that's a betrayal of all our trust."

"Don't think of it like that. That, there, is a formula for eternal conflict."

"But Jonas...," I interrupted.

To me he said, "I'll talk to you about that later." Then back to Amazin', "The trust I gotta take care of is to the common soldier that I don't stick they neck out needlessly. Fact is, we win this war by sitting out. I don't like to put it that way, but sometimes we gotta demand some understanding. If you can get behind me for the sake of your living brothers, then that's where we going to find our strength. Take pride in doing what's right even against your own inclination. It may be a hard pill to swallow, but choke it down if you have to."

And later, in a private conference, Jonas said to me, "We don't ever let anyone dictate our conflicts for us."

39

"Put together that heist you told me about."

"What heist?"

"When you said you could put together a big robbery to get us some money."

"I never said that."

"Well, whatever you claim you said, do it. The boys need some action."

"I don't know what you're talking about. I don't got no plan, and if getting big money was just as easy as sitting down one day and saying 'How can we do it...?' shit, everyone would be rich."

"I don't care. Be innovative."

I brainstormed ideas for any kind of out-of-the-ordinary plan that might net us some money. My basic thinking was that good heists attack weak targets, exploit trust, and are unexpected. The problem was that every idea that leapt to mind, at first, was a strongarm attack or involved weapons, or it was otherwise illegal by the standards of our click, or else it was too common, so security would be strong and we couldn't get an edge. Still, I kicked around anything I could think of:

What if we rob a museum? Jewelry? Art? Some elaborate con? A gambling scam? Who's a soft target? Can we blackmail someone? All of this was dangerous, obvious, done before, and outside our areas of expertise. I didn't think we could pull off any of it. *Arson for hire? Forgery? Fake gold. No, what? Investment scam? Blackmail? Thought of that. Who? Fake drugs. Toys? High-seas piracy. What the fuck?*

I decided to sleep on it. I did a lot of sleeping that week.

Then I took a survey.

"Who do you know that's got money...? Where's a soft target...? Where are people gullible...? What have you picked up...? What have you heard...? Is there anything you thought of before but rejected because you thought it was a bad idea? Could one of those ideas really be good?"

I entertained a thousand crazy ideas, until I settled on one I thought would work.

I'd never heard of a robbery of a university bookstore, but some of the boys I spoke to who had relatives or friends that went to college said that sometimes *tons* of money flow through those places at the start of a semester. I mean literally eight-hundred, nine-hundred, a thousand students—sometimes many more—each bringing in hundreds of dollars on the same day. Some bring checks, but with the rush on the checkout lines on a crowded day, and all the hassle checking I.D. and shit, cash is not unusual for a lot of students. But they're not guarded closely like banks or liquor stores because there's not much of a precedent for crime there.

I spent a lot of time researching, including asking more questions to more people and making several visits to the library. I was searching out a suitable location: some East-Bumfuck college-town considered safe and middle class up around the great lakes, with student enrollment in the upper thousands or tens of thousands, having a start in the first week of September. I found it.

An armed hold-up wouldn't fly with our click rules, and it would probably have been stupid and dangerous anyway. You just never know what could go wrong with hundreds of civilians on site, plus the outrage at such a crime would fuel an interstate manhunt. But I figured the Pollyanna idealism and gullibility in a town full of college-educated liberal white folks meant a simple con could get the money. So I combined my idea for a target with a scheme I'd carried around in my head for several years until I'd almost forgot it.

The basic idea was we'd make a fake night-deposit for a bank, install it, and get the local suckers to drop they money in there, then take it.

The target location had a university whose classes were scheduled to start on the first Wednesday in September, and whose bookstore had announced they would be open on Labor Day—an unusual move designed to accommodate late-arriving students since the holiday came early that year. On Labor Day, of course, all bank locations would be closed.

I tried to think of everything we'd need, and I put together a team. Besides myself, there was Solid, Clip, Terrible, and three of the newer soldiers who had picked up some experience and skills: Damian "Flip" Broadus, Galen "Tongue" Johnson, and Joe "Fortress" Johnson (not related to Tongue). I sent Flip and Fortress ahead to buy sweatshirts and any gear that would help them pass for students. Terrible went with them to help gather information on what went on in the store. I used channels that Amazin' had negotiated to get us a fake bank-guard uniform that would fit Ivan. We arranged to rent a truck with a lift-gate and dolly, and a few other tools, using fake I.D.s. We had to plan a way to make the I.D.s right up close to the time of the heist so we could match the names to stolen credit cards we'd buy off of another connection.

Clip, Solid, and I groomed our hair, got manicures, bought leather loafers, and got us some clean, pressed, innocuous-looking preppy clothes, plus windbreakers to throw on and keep our outfits clean anytime we had to roll around in bushes or shit like that. Tongue got a white polo shirt, black slacks, and a green apron to pass for a grocery store clerk.

There was more stuff to gather, of course, on top of which we needed two (cheap, used) cars legally registered, with additional fake plates to put on when close to the scene of the crime.

But the most important thing was to manufacture the fake drop-safe deposit slot that we would install in front of the real depository. It had to look good and trustworthy, it had to be quick to install but look and feel like it was built right into the structure of the wall and bolted into the concrete, and it had to be the right dimensions, color, and material to match the design of the target bank. Terrible and his boys observed the habits of the bookstore management for a while, to indentify which bank they deposited with, and then they went to take pictures and measurements. They discovered that the bank didn't have drive-through services, and the depository was mounted on the side of the bank where customers had to get up out they cars and walk a few yards to use it. After concluding they information-gathering mission, they came back down to help with our preparations.

We had a shop we could work with, so we got a very heavy, mostly solid concrete column with just a narrow chute leading to a trap at the bottom, and there was a hollow space at the back that would go over and cover the bank's real deposit slot. The whole thing was constructed with lead weights in the concrete near the base, and a gasket was affixed to the bottom to prevent rocking or sliding when it rested on slightly rough concrete pavement. A real, solid-steel drop-safe door was installed in the front face of the column near the top, designed to drop straight down into the chute. The money trap below had one soft wood panel on the side, lightly covered with concrete and a layer of painted plaster to match the rest of the dummy-depository. This ensured there'd be no visible door or suspicious looking features on the outside of the column, but when we were ready we could kick in the panel and empty out the cash fast without having to move anything or waste time.

When the time came, we drove up in two sub-teams. It was the weekend before Labor Day. Car A was Solid, Clip, and Flip. Clip was the main driver. Car B was me, Terrible, Fortress, and Tongue, with Tongue driving. As we got close to our destination that Saturday, we took Fortress in to the rental garage to get the truck, which he drove on from there.

So far, everything was smooth.

On Sunday night, kids were partying on the university campus. At the bank, nothing was going on.

I posted Clip and Flip parked in they cars at two intersections in opposite directions from the bank, to lookout. They were in radio contact with the rest of us waiting in the truck. At two AM they radioed in the all-clear, and fortress drove us into the bank's lot. We wheeled the column onto the gate, lowered it, and rolled it out to where we would mount it. Fortress was handy with these kinds of things, so he applied the sealant to the gasket while we did our best to sweep, wash, and clean the pavement where it would be seated. It took four of us lifting to tilt the column up from its side onto its base and we had to rock and pivot it a bit to get it flush with the wall. We did accidentally put a small scratch on the wall near the bottom-right-back corner of our column, but I didn't think it looked too obvious or suspicious. Finally we got a little caulk into the narrow space where column met wall, and everyone but Flip got into the truck and drove away. Flip did final clean up and applied a little paint to the scratch. Then he caught a ride with Clip.

We got some rest at the motel until 11:00 AM the next day. Around that time, I sent Fortress to make his first trip to the bookstore to check out how business was flowing, while Tongue, Terrible, and I cruised past the bank just to see everything looked kosher.

As expected, no one had tampered with our drop-safe, and there were no customers around. It was too early to expect any businesses to make deposits unless someone came in the predawn hours from an all-night gas station.

At 1:00 PM, my team and I cruised over to the bank again.

We saw someone getting into his car in the bank parking lot and driving off. We circled the block across the way, came back around, and parked on a side street where we could get a view. Twenty minutes later, another bank customer arrived.

I picked up my telescope to get a better view of the transaction.

"What's up with that? Are you a pirate?"

"Shut up. Look, he's putting his deposit bag in."

"And?"

"It's like everything's normal. He just dropped it in, now he's going back to his car. Looks calm and unsuspicious."

"I can see that with my bare eyes."

"I just want to get a close look to see they faces."

"Binoculars can do that."

"I don't like looking with two eyes."

"You don't look with two eyes every day?"

"I mean with binoculars. I don't like them."

"But..."

"You live to fuck with me, don't you?"

We got a radio call from Clip:

"Hey, the bookstore guy is on his way."

"Yeah?"

"Yeah. Assistant manager, I think. Fortress spotted him coming out and getting in his car with a leather bag."

"What's he look like?"

Just then, another customer was arriving in the bank lot.

"White guy, goatee, receding hairline, white collared shirt."

"Cool."

The customer who arrived was a thin, older white man, not fitting the manager's description. As he walked to the depository, another car pulled into the lot. A kind of heavy, full-figured Latina.

The white guy looked at the deposit-slot, put his money in, started walking away, but then paused and looked back suspiciously. He walked back to the depository and looked at it more closely, opened the door to check the money had gone down, and closed it again. When the Latina woman walked up, he started talking to her, and she chatted with him.

"Damn!" I said. "Tongue, it's time to play shill."

Terrible and I hopped out the car. Tongue started the engine and drove over to the bank lot. While the two customers were having a conversation, he got out in his grocer's assistant outfit and walked over with his own deposit bag. The two talked to him a little bit, and he talked back.

Ivan and I were standing, peeking around the corner to see what would happen. Ivan had his bank-guard uniform on, but we hadn't made any use of it yet.

Tongue went ahead and put his deposit bag in while the other two watched, then walked over to his car. Following his example, the Latina made her own deposit. The white guy shrugged a little. He seemed baffled.

While Tongue was pulling out the lot, and the Latina was starting her car, *another* car arrived. The old white dude walked over to the driver of this car and started talking to him. He pointed over to the depository, then chatted some more.

"Fuck."

The conversation went on for a while, then the older white dude shrugged his shoulders again and walked back to his own car.

Tongue came around the block, parked, and we got in.

"What happened?"

"That dude was telling the lady he wasn't sure but it seemed strange someone had done some construction work over the holiday weekend. Something seemed different since he came on Saturday. I just told them 'Boss said take the money to the bank and come back quick.' I deposited and left."

"Good job."

"Well," said Ivan, "he got us one customer, but the busybody's still fucking around. You want me to get over there?"

"Nah. You suddenly arriving while a customer is sitting in his car will seem weird. Damn, what's he going to do?"

By now the busybody had driven away. The newly arrived customer got out his car. He was the assistant bookstore manager, for sure, but he didn't carry the leather bag. He walked over and looked at the depository, then turned and looked around him. I think he spotted our car where we were parked.

"This don't look good."

He got back in his car and drove away without making the deposit.

"Oh fuck. That's it. We're done."

"Think someone will call the police?"

"Maybe, but let's go."

Tongue drove us out of there.

I radioed over to the other team to get Flip into the store to watch carefully what went on, and they should all be ready to book if something further went wrong. Twenty minutes later I got the message: the assistant manager had returned to the store, walked in with his leather bag, went back to the store-office, then got on the floor and continued business normally.

"Did he talk to the manager or other clerks where you could hear him?"

"No. Or, just to say something normal like, 'Jimmy get over to the third register.'"

"What you think, boss?" said Ivan.

"*Now* you call me boss."

"Anyway, any chance they going to come back and make the deposit later?"

"Very unlikely. As in no chance."

"You want me to go grab what's in the depository?"

"Not yet. We'll cruise by in a few hours and see if anyone's tampered with it. But hell! I'm not giving up on that bookstore money. We're getting it, or my name's not Orville Redenbacher."

"It isn't."

"Anyway..." I got back on the radio. "Clip, we got a job for you. I'll give you the details. Let's meet at IHOP."

We got everyone together. We had our two cars. The truck was elsewhere. Clip came over to my car for a quick conference.

"Alright, listen. We need every tool you can get that might be useful. Sledgehammers. Heavy ones. Axes, prybars—long ones. Drills. Tarps. Everything."

"Stores are closed. There's nothing open but a few groceries, restaurants, and a movie theater."

"Yeah, but I count on your skills. You got hours. Get out, drive around, find any construction sites that might have tools around. Try private tool sheds if you have to. Take one or two boys."

"Alright, cool, I can do that."

"I have no doubt."

He hopped out, but then I called him back.

"Fuck. Hey, wait!"

He came back.

"No, scrap it, we'll put other boys on it for now. I need you for something else. You got your car kit?"

"Well... you told me to keep the car clean in case we got searched or something."

"And?"

"And I brought it anyway."

"You know, I fucking knew it! But no violation this time. I need you to get us a pickup truck. Best you can do would be steal it from the campus. If kids still partying, no one'll even notice it's gone, but if they do notice, that'll just give campus security something to fuss about and keep they eyes off the bookstore."

"That's why you're the Brain."

"Also, we need tarps."

"Got it."

After a little costume change, Terrible took Tongue on the tool-gathering mission while Fortress brought Clip back over to the campus for car-thieving purposes. Solid and I ate pancakes.

Fortress and Clip met us back at the motel a few hours later. Clip had secured the pickup truck as requested. Fortress took me on a cruise past the bank for one more checkup. The depository was still in place, and there were no cops or security in sight. We waited and watched for an hour.

I got a radio-call from Solid. Most of the tools we needed had been acquired, and a couple of the boys were over casing out the bookstore again. The store closed up. The assistant had come out with no leather bag. The manager left and locked up.

"Don't look like they taking the money out the store tonight."

To be sure, Fortress and I sat watching the bank for another half an hour. Nothing doing. We left.

At 11:00 PM, we went back to the bank for the last time. This time it was me, Tongue, and Ivan again. Everything was still quiet and normal. We pulled into the lot. Ivan got out in his uniform. He walked over to the depository, didn't bother with any hesitation or looking around, kicked in the panel, and quickly scooped all the deposit bags out into a duffel.

Post-midnight, we were all back at the motel with everything we needed, ready to go.

With the big truck, we drove over to the parking lot behind the bookstore. Clip was parked several blocks away in the pickup, off on a side street, where we also parked our other cars.

At the bookstore, everyone got out the truck, and I took the driver's seat. I put on the seatbelt. I had a motorcycle helmet that Clip had got me. From the greatest distance possible within the lot, I took the truck in reverse to about thirty miles per hour and crashed it through a wall that didn't have any solid columns behind it. The truck penetrated about two and a half feet in, and the crash shook me hard.

I drove out of the breech, which was still not completely smashed through, then went in reverse for a second time, hit it solid, and came all the way through the wall, blasting books and shelves out of the way.

I got out of the breech once more. I was hurt and winded. I clambered out of the truck.

We all rushed through the opening. Solid and Fortress carried tools. Flip stayed outside to lower the truck's gate, and then started clearing away as much rubble and trash as possible. Happily the lift-gate on the truck still worked, or we'd probably have been fucked.

We used the sledge-hammers to smash down the office door. It came down pretty quick. Terrible and Tongue cleared out the wreckage of the door, and then helped Flip to clear a path for a dolly from office to truck. They were heaving the scattered books and fragments of shattered shelves everywhere.

We turned on all the lights because there was no point in trying to hide our presence. We were raising enough noise it sounded like a small war in progress.

In the office, we found the safe. Terrible wheeled the small dolly to just outside the door. It was too wide to bring in. We tried to tilt the safe up with pry-bars, but it wouldn't budge.

"It's bolted to the floor, or the wall!"

"Smash that fucker with everything you got!"

Solid and Fortress used they heavy sledges to smite the bottom of the safe. They hit it a dozen times quick, and the clamor was something you could feel in your bones.

Ivan started singing!

"*Stick to the promise, girl, uh... you made me! Wouldn't go get married till uh... I gone free!*"

"Come on, man!"

"*I gone free, lordy... I gone free! Wouldn't go get married till uh... I gone free!*"

"Shut up. That song's too slow!"

"It's moving!"

"Get the pry under it."

The safe pried up. The concrete that the bolts went into was pulverized. We flipped the safe on its side onto a blanket that we brought to reduce friction. Five of us pulled, pushed, and got that safe as far as the door. Then we used the pry-bars to flip it again and get it on the dolly.

We were rolling the dolly across the store when Flip met us inside and said, "There's a cop out there."

A couple of us looked out. It was a campus cop looking at us from a distance out in the lot.

"Hey, what are you doing in there!?" he challenged.

We went about our business. We got the dolly onto the lift gate, then most of us ran out and stood on the side of the truck opposite where the campus cop was standing, about sixty yards away. He was looking at us nervous. As Solid came out of the store, he hurled his sledgehammer at the cop with all his might. The cop scooted out of the way at the last second and the hammer hit a car.

Flip operated the gate, and it slowly lifted the safe.

I saw a lot of books were heaped inside the truck.

"What the fuck is that?"

"Some of these books are like a hundred dollars a pop. Maybe more."

"But what are we going to do with them?"

The campus cop had a gun. He shot at us.

"Whip another hammer!"

Ivan handed the second sledgehammer to Solid, and he hurled it at the cop.

By now the gate was fully lifted, we scrambled into the truck—Fortress had started the engine—and we drove away. The cop gave up shooting. We were crammed like clowns in a clown-car rolling all over each other with Flip hanging halfway out the window.

At our designated meeting point, we used the lift gate to lower the safe to a level where we could wheel it into the pickup. Flip and Tongue started shoveling some of the books into the truck too, but I stopped them as it wasn't worth our time. We abandoned the rental truck.

Fortress drove the pickup. I went along with him so we could take turns driving and never have to stop except for gas. The rest of them piled into two other cars. Somewhere along the line, they ditched the fake plates.

✌

We got back home without any further complications.

Sammy shouted, "You are heistors!"

When we'd had a chance to rest, the next day, Tongue met me and handed me a book.

"Look what I got you, Brain."

It was a copy of Frederick Douglass's *My Bondage and My Freedom*. I hadn't read that one yet.

"Wow. That's really cool of you."

"I knew you liked him."

"You get one for yourself?"

"No. Maybe we can share it around."

"How come you got only one?"

"Well... you know, they didn't have that many on the shelves to begin with."

"Right. That's something to think about."

I had to be a little cautious for a while because I caught a whiplash from driving through that wall despite precautions, and two days later I had my neck in a brace. It made me feel a little stupid.

Tallying up the loot, we had $9,800 and change from the deposit bags in the fake drop-safe. We had eighteen three-volume sets of *The Feynman Lectures on Physics*, and fourteen copies of *A Concise Introduction to Logic*, which might have been worth money to university students but had no value for us. And we had that clunky safe full of who-knew-what.

The pickup truck we stole got us enough in the resale to more than pay for all the expenses of our trip, including manufacturing costs, props, tools, transport, etcetera, plus a couple hundred dollars extra profit. That was cool.

But it took about a week for a contact Bank had made among the Boulevards to hook us up with a safecracker. We paid him $600 to drill the safe for us, since the job was completely risk-free, working in a shop with no chance of getting caught and no entitlement to any share.

While he was drilling, Ivan cracked up laughing.

"What?"

"What if there's shit in there?" he said.

"What?"

"I mean, what if, just to fuck with us, the manager didn't put any money in there, and he took a shit in the safe?"

"You're fucking retarded."

But we were all laughing.

When the safe came open it was $92,000. Not life-changing money, maybe, but a good payday, and the best single heist we'd pulled off in over two years. It was something to celebrate—and we did—right after we burned all the personal checks, finance records, time-sheets, pay-slips, schedules, and other evidence along with all the unsellable textbooks. Then lid-off time was here again!

Jonas was happy, not just for the money we brought in, but because the adventure stimulated the boys to get back into the spirit of the struggle, taking charge of things, and not always thinking about warring with enemies. It gave us a chance to laugh and exchange stories and get everybody's perspective on things.

"What's been happening while I was away?" I asked.

"For once, nothing. Things have been normal and mostly easy-going."

"Let's stay that way."

40.

THERE WAS STARTING to be some pressure on us to stay out of Brandywine Park during daylight hours because the area was becoming more "family friendly." Moms were taking they little kids to play in the park more. It made the place look better, but it complicated things. Technically, Brandywine Park was south of Yost *Street*, but we didn't consider it part of the South-Brehms *area* because white humans didn't go there except for teens who sometimes got in our games, and that wasn't much. It had always been our spot. But now it was like humans forgot the blood that once stained the concrete. It wasn't that long ago.

Seeing kids run and play and drink apple juice with they moms is cool. But now there was starting to be some white moms and white kids coming too. What's the difference? I got nothing against white moms and white kids. But, well, whether it's a coincidence or not, that was when cops starting hassling us if we were seen drinking and smoking in the park, or playing dice. We couldn't raise a ruckus. We couldn't have any fun. I mean, we *could*, but it always led to some kind of complaint.

Fair enough, let the children have they fun. But one night— at eleven o'clock PM!—a cop cruiser pulled up near the park and shined its lights in at us.

"Clear the park!" said the voice on the megaphone.

"What!? Fuck that."

"Why? Why we gotta clear the park?"

"Go home, the park's closed."

"Closed?"

A cop got out of the car and walked up the path towards us as we got whatever cash was out into our pockets.

"Did you just hear us telling you clear the park?"

"Yeah, but…"

"Don't come back here. Go home."

"But why? What we do?"

"Park's closed."

"What closed? What are you talking about?"

"See that sign?"

He pointed to a sign we could hardly see in the dark. He then shined a flashlight on it. It was a slab of wood painted green, on a rusty pipe tilted at a weird angle coming out the ground. The lettering was raised on the surface, but most of the white paint was peeled off. Still, we could read it. Among other things, it said "This park closes at dusk."

"How old is that sign? From the 1950s? That sign's been there my whole life, I think, and nobody once ever told me, 'You gotta go home, park's closed.'"

"Your raising's not my business. The park is closed."

"It's never been a problem."

"It's a problem now. You can go home, or you can go to jail for vagrancy."

We all went off.

"Vagrancy!? You think I live here?"

"You just told him 'go home.' How you tell him 'go home' you think he's a vagrant?"

"What is this? You wouldn't even walk in this park alone among fifteen black kids except you know who we are, and we don't fuck with police. We don't make trouble for no one."

"I'm telling you keep the peace, go home, and if you start fussing like this, you'll soon see the riot police coming through to clear this park."

"Who complained? Who's complaining? This is ridiculous. You never heard us making any real trouble in this park."

"This is a public space. We the public."

"No," said the cop. "You got that half right. This is a public space, and I'm here representing the community interests. Guess what? The community doesn't want to hear you messing around here at all hours."

"I don't know where you just drove in from, but you're not a part of our community."

The cop got on his radio.

"Call backup."

"Nah, nah. We'll leave. But you don't gotta be messing with us when we make no fuss..."

We left.

We made sure to be there again the next night, and the next night, and there was no trouble those nights, but on the third night some police cars pulled up together and five cops came in on foot and ran us out.

We returned again.

Several days after that, seven cars pulled up around all the sides of the park, with lights flashing, and we knew shit was serious.

Quite-Right picked up a rock and said he was going to whip it at a cop.

Jonas told him, "Put it down."

We ditched our blades in the bushes, and marched out of the park single file with our hands in the air. As we came out to where the lights were brightest, we saw cops had they guns pulled. They commanded us to sit along the curb. Then, one by one, they frisked and cuffed Jonas, me, Solid, Flower, Keychain, a new soldier named Charles "Ponder" Sneed, and a tourist in our game who had no click affiliation. Because they targeted two O.G.s and a captain, we figured they were well educated on who we were, but some of the other arrests seemed arbitrary. They let everyone else go.

We were read our rights, and we were told we were being charged with disorderly conduct, criminal nuisance, and promoting gambling. We were released the following morning after paying bail according to the schedule. We bailed the tourist out along with us, told him not to worry about it, and assured him we'd cover any legal expenses. He'd never been in jail before, and he was scared. Us backing him up restored some of his confidence, and I think it sent the right message.

We were back in the park within the week, but only at night. In the next few months, there were two more instances where the cops came and told us to disperse, but there were no more arrests, and after that the cops didn't come around anymore. We never knew when they would, though.

༃

One time we were dicing in the daytime in a small lot on Ulrich St. with some suckers in attendance. It had become our new daytime spot. Anthony "Hot-Sauce" Baptiste, another of our soldiers, was apprenticing with Hops to learn See-Low skills, and today he was running real hot. He paused a moment during the game and sent a baby on an errand to pick him up a forty-ounce at the bodega. Then, while fading $30 of Sammy's $100 stake, Hot-Sauce rolled a 4-5-6 against Sammy's point of 5.

Sammy pulled him out of the circle, quick, and everyone took notice.

"Hey, you playing left-handed!?"

Sammy slapped his face hard.

"Mala, you get in this!" Sammy said.

I came over to confront Hot-Sauce.

"You caught him at it?"

"Damn fucking right, I did."

Hot-Sauce just looked shook up like he didn't know what to say or how to deny. Sammy punched him in the sternum.

I got behind him while he was trying to edge away, grabbed his elbows, then spun one-eighty to my left and tripped up his feet so he stumbled and fell into the road.

"Don't fuck with our game! You get up and get out."

He got hisself up and backed away across the street mumbling something about he didn't do anything. Just then the baby returned from the store with Hot-Sauce's forty, and I called him over.

"Give me that."

And I hurled the heavy glass bottle in the brown paper bag across the street at Hot-Sauce. He tried to dodge, but it hit his leg just over the side of his knee and then fragmented on the pavement. He was hobbling when he ran out of there.

"Don't come back, neither!"

The baby had seventeen dollars and some coins in his hand.

"What about the change?"

I took it and threw it back where we were dicing. The game resumed.

"Next person rolls 1-2-3 takes it as a consolation prize."

The suckers who observed this scene got a really positive impression that we guarded our games against all cheaters and dishonesty. It helped our reputation that we disciplined members of our own click. Only thing is, that wasn't what happened at all, and as you know, cheating suckers was what we were all about.

No. We had an old tradition that when gambling, you keep your own private funds in your front-right pocket. Company bankroll stays in your left pocket, in your hand, in your jacket, or whatever, but you segregate it from personal money. We got a little lax with it sometimes, but you had to keep your accounting straight somehow. So if a dude needed to spend some cash while gambling on behalf of the click, if he spent money out his hand or bankroll because of convenience, he had to refund it out his personal money as soon as possible, visibly, or signal the senior in attendance that he's taking a loan. If not, you're stealing.

Hot-Sauce had handed off a twenty from his bankroll like

it was normal, and didn't refund it. When he collected from Sammy, that was a perfect opportunity to use a catch-phrase like "Let's keep it rolling" if he couldn't get his finances straight right away. But he didn't do that. And it's stupid because we got a quartermastor, we got beer quotas, and O.G.s and captains take care of they boys. Nobody goes thirsty if you're just straight about what you want. But who knows where that seventeen dollars change would've went?

Hot-Sauce came in to the clubhouse that night to hand over the bankroll he'd collected, and to complain publicly to Jonas that we had abused him.

"It's not right I'm being made an example of. I'm pulling in money for the click, and just a little slip, and now all this drama for nothing."

"If they're treating you like an example, then *be* an example. You've been schooled, right? If we let you slip, who else is allowed to slip?"

"Come on. You know it was a mistake. And there are other minor violators."

"You are minor violator!" shouted Sammy, to our general merriment.

"Take four days off," said Jonas. "Just don't come around. Don't talk to any of the brothers and don't be seen."

"I'm short of cash..."

"I'm sure someone'll front you. If not, beg quarters downtown... no, don't come in for a hug from me—not yet."

"You are guiltor!" said Sammy.

"Get out."

In our later conversation, Jonas talked to me about the conditions in the gang:

"The younger generations constantly got to be taught the core values. We can't let them fall into bad ways."

Hot-Sauce served his four days banishment, and when he came back, he got his hug from Thayne and everything was cool. Jonas kept his distance but politely acknowledged Hot-Sauce's return.

We judge the sin, but not the sinner.

41.

JONAS AND I, and Lettuce too, were hanging out at James's again. Thayne and Prez still didn't like that place for whatever reason, I don't know, so they didn't come.

Jonas was getting philosophical, and in our conversation he turned to James behind the bar.

"Uncle James. Give us some wisdom."

"Hey listen," says Uncle James. "When I was your age, I was a young fool."

"Mmm hmm."

"You know what happens when a young fool grows up?"

"What?"

"You get an old fool. I got no wisdom for you."

While we were laughing, this black kid I don't know and never heard of comes in and approaches us at the bar.

"Excuse me," he says.

"Yeah?" says Jonas.

"Listen, I got a message."

We looked at him harshly.

"Calvin Trice wants to meet with you."

"And? How'd you come out here looking for us?"

"The only thing I got to say is Calvin wants to meet you, and he couldn't reach you on the phone."

"Fuck no. Is he outside?"

"He's not far."

"I told him I'm changing my number."

"Well, listen." The kid put a card on the bar. "You can call me on that number and anything you got to say I'll put you in touch with Calvin. He sincerely wants to hear from you."

"Why?"

"That's not for me to say."

"And who you? If I'm supposed to call you."

"I'm Scott Green. They call me Red."

"So you're Red Green?"

"That's right."

Jonas got up a bit abruptly.

"Hey, you look familiar."

"I'm a Ronin."

"There still Ronins?"

"Not many. I'm one. I gotta go."

Kid left.

"This world spins my head around sometimes."

Hardcore had a cousin on the other side of town who associated from time to time with an F.O.M.-West set. We sometimes turned to him for information on what went on in the Grogans and other Lubb factions. Since no information was coming any other way, Hardcore was sent out to investigate and report back.

He reported to the O.G.s when we were in council.

"What you learn?" Jonas asked.

"Civil war's opened up. Rudy Simms got his cap peeled. Everyone thinks Wally Jackson ordered it. Police are all over it. And meanwhile, they product dried up. They been begging other Fams to lend or sell them product, but no one wants to touch it."

"And what's behind that."

"No one's talking about it, or not so my cousin would know. I think I just told you everything I know."

"You think?"

"Yeah."

"Alright, it's serious. Calvin Trice has got me curious. I gotta talk to him. Mala, you still in?"

"Do you doubt? Trice and I are getting friendly!"

"What about me?" asked President. "I'm not feeling my O.G.-ness lately."

"Come along, why not. Uh, thanks, Hardcore, we gotta talk now, right?"

"Yeah, cool."

"Thayne? If we come back in caskets, don't cry too much at our funerals, alright?"

Thayne's expression showed he didn't see this as a joke. He had a tendency towards humorlessness at the most awkward times.

⋟

Through Red Green, we got in contact with Trice and invited him—on a one-time-only basis—to visit us at James's bar. "Since you know where we hang at anyway," said Jonas. "But after tonight, you know it's our spot, and you and your associates are not to come sneaking around or we'll take it as an act of war."

Trice came alone and looked completely self-assured.

"Boys, it's fucking great to see you. Listen, I'm just going to tell you so there's no mystery: I'm back."

"Back."

"Yeah, and so I wanted to be a good neighbor and check in and make sure you and I are still friends."

"Let's call it friendly acquaintances."

"That's good enough."

"But what do you mean by being 'back.' What's happened? We heard Simms is done."

"Yeah, that's true. He wasn't a reliable guy, but you know he was good, I mean essentially good. It's sad."

"You're not being sarcastic?"

"No. Can I be sarcastic about a brother's death!? Every time it happens, it makes a brother pause."

"Fuck, I can't read you. Seriously, you could be leveling me, I don't know."

"Jonas?" I said.

"What, Afro? Don't be elbowing me."

"I'm just saying..." And I gestured at Trice like to say *Let the brother continue.* (Seriously, Jonas told me before the meeting not to reveal any doubt or uncertainty, and here he's telling me 'don't elbow me.')

Trice picked up his cue:

"Just between you and me and the denizens of Earth, Wally Jackson's dead too."

"Huh."

"Yeah, man. Not many humans know this yet, but it'll be coming around soon enough. Thing is, Jackson was the first to draw blood, and that was his undoing, see? You was probably right to sit out on this conflict, you showed some savvy."

"Your flattery disturbs me," said Jonas.

"Anyway," Trice continued, "the whole point is just to secure my rear and give you the security of knowing I've got no plots and no concerns that conflict with yours. As for wanting your payment in blood, well, you got two O.G.s, once friends of mine. One's had his funeral already. The other's not going to have a funeral, but he's just as buried as the other."

"You cold. No heads on sticks though?"

"I don't got them. I had nothing to do with it. The whole plot collapsed on itself, but I'm here to pick up the pieces; I got enough support to put together a skeleton crew, and the old Ronins... you know, some of them still miss they homeland, but I'm holding them off. I got them well under my thumb. They're going to be fresh blood in the crew. They'll be joining the remnants of the old-guard that I still have trust in. There're still some good boys among the Grogans I can put back in shape."

"What about the outlaws?" asked President.

"There's not going to be any outlaws. I'm having an amnesty.

But you know, some boys just run off on they own. They give up because things got tough, or they don't trust me, I don't know. I let them go. War is not on the agenda right now, I've had enough of that. But here's the thing. I'm telling you how things fell out, and I'm giving you my assurances, and you know, we're not going to mess with you unnecessarily. But what I'm demanding, and this is non-negotiable, is that we stick to the old borders, which means exactly that you don't have any influence, direct or indirect, on the business north of Silver. Nothing that goes on there is your business. On your side, that's your business. You got all the security you like. You can be do-gooders or do-badders, fuck if I care."

"Are you going to tell us what happened to Jackson?"

"Yeah, if you like stories."

"Who don't?"

"It's real simple. The guy who handles most of our supply is a real paranoid motherfucker with heavy connections, but I always got on with him. You know, we both understood the business relationship. But with me out of the picture, tensions ratcheted up, and then warring within the set, you know... ordering Simms's death was just dumb. Not that Jackson had any better alternatives except maybe just to run. So, someone who was in on whatever meeting occurred where the hit on Simms was planned reached the point he was going to collaborate with the cops."

"Who?"

"Do I know?"

"You sound like you know."

"I don't know. But the cops were asking every kind of question..."

"And this you *do* know."

"Look, I'm just telling you what I put together. I got sources, but what do I trust, what do I not? What do people tell me, what do they hide? When it's written up in the history books, this is how it's going to go. It looked like an arrest for Jackson was going to come, maybe now, maybe in six months, but someone was talking or was rumored to be talking, and the boys all had murderous gleams in they eyes and hunger in they bellies because suddenly the drug supply got cut off. Our man, who shall go unnamed, was not going to get connected to anyone in case an untrustworthy motherfucker like Jackson was going to talk. Got it?"

"Yeah."

"Do I need to go on?"

"Are you thirsty? Uncle James! L.G.C. wants a hookup!"

"Sounds dangerous. But okay, if you're imbibing some weird potion, I'll join you. So, yeah, the rest is kind of obvious if you think about it. Jackson's dead. He fled, you know. Got cash of course and ran. And someone knew what bus, and that info got relayed to Mr. So-and-so who took care of business."

"Did you have anything to do with that information relay?"

"You think someone's going to trust that info to me? I was on the sidelines like you, you know, waiting for shit to happen. I just happen to be in a position after the fact to ask the right questions to the right people. You know, in exchange for a chance to get things straight again."

"So actually you know exactly who the informant was, and you're keeping him around because it serves you."

"Well... I'm not saying any of that. Maybe some associate with our source is more informed than any rat within our set. Amnesty don't extend to someone who cooperates with authorities. Like... you know."

"Another unofficial burial. I got you. It's cool. We knew you were a devious motherfucker. You earn your reputation. And all's fine, serious. It's not like we needed complications. You keep your count, and do whatever business you gotta. But: Not only are you not going to do business anywhere in or around *our* count, and that includes the south-side-of-Silver businesses that run our numbers, including the new Shazaam, but I need more. You gotta turn away some customers that might come across shopping from the corner."

"That's not realistic."

"Suddenly you want to talk about realism, when I was ready to swallow that fairytale you telling."

"Truth is stranger than fiction, man. You tell him, Mala. You're the skeptic; he's supposed to be more trusting."

"No, I'm the gullible one."

"Shit, I can't keep you guys straight."

"Anyway," says Jonas. "You can just tell your boys to quit supplying a few addicts that walk over your way from out our count. Just... scale back or something."

"That... Come on, really?"

"How much they spend with you? It can't be much?"

"You'd be surprised."

"But you know it'll take years to equal how much you put on just one damned sports bet."

"I knew you'd be asking something for that!"

"Why the fuck not? I'm not asking for money, now, I'm asking for people."

"Fuck, alright, why not."

"Just smack they faces. When they come shopping, tell your dealers smack they faces and say 'Go home to your kids.'"

"Shit, Jonas, you must've had a fucked up childhood." Pause. "Sorry, I didn't mean to joke."

Four days later, Red Green came walking into Jack-Rabbit Corner talking about he's got another message from Trice. Boys made him wait on the corner until I could come out and meet him.

"What's your message?"

"Can I talk to Cloud?"

"Talk to me and I'll pass it on."

"Alright. Calvin wants to tell you that the whole turning away customers thing isn't going to work out. It's just likely to cause some disagreement in the future, and he don't want that. So he's got another proposal."

"Yeah?"

"He gave me a list to give to you. It's the ten most notorious fiends from your count that buy from us. You can work things out with them however you want, but if you can't stop them from shopping in our count, then we no longer responsible."

"Sounds like he's reneging."

"Nah, he just wants your agreement on this. You know, this way, if we're quits, there won't be any haggling over who's accountable. No one has to be checking up on anyone."

"That makes some sense, but it wasn't what we agreed to. I'll get you a message with Cloud's response."

"Also, to seal the deal and say we're all done with it, Calvin wants to send you over six cases of whiskey."

"Cool. Well, I gotta talk to Jonas. Can you be back here in forty minutes."

"Yeah. I'll come and go."

Jonas approved of the deal. I went back to meet Red Green, same corner.

"Alright, we're settled."

He handed over the note with the list of addicts, and we loaded the whiskey from his truck to one of ours.

"One last thing," I said. "Cloud says not to send you as a messenger anymore. Get a new guy."

"Yeah, that'll be fine."

We distributed one bottle of scotch to each soldier, captain, and O.G. in the click, and we kept the rest in a reserve at the clubhouse. (At this point we had a real clubhouse, separate from anyone's living quarters. O.G.s still congregated sometimes at Jonas's.) Notably, this one gesture made more of an impression things were really settled than anything had gone before. We sipped calm, breathed easy. Only Amazin' remained agitated. He slipped away a few days after. His disappearance was a big loss, especially to those of us who knew him so long, and I figured he left because he felt we'd betrayed him. I can understand that, but we had a different perspective on things.

42.

Ten North-Brehms Fiends From the S·M·F Count

EMMA JAIKARAN–From Crystal Street near Freya. She got three kids she's always talking about.

LUCY WILLIAMS–From somewhere on Lee Street. Lives with her husband but he's a drunk and don't know about her habits. Has been known to turn tricks from time to time, usually in the early morning on the other side of the bridge.

BYRON BYRD–Has a mole over his left eyebrow and lives somewhere in Jack-Rabbit Corner area. Has a kind of humming tic.

IRIS JENKINS–Doesn't seem like a fiend, but comes around all the time. Quiet. Her brother Ron talked about her once to a coworker related to one of our boys.

MIGUEL–Doesn't look Latin. Short. Dark. We don't know his family name or where he's from exactly, but he's an unmistakable fiend. Glassy-eyed. Stoic face.

STU–Real nervous type. Makes others nervous. I think he plays one of your numbers games regularly and we've seen him come and go from the bodega on Fitzsimmons on your side of Silver.

"BILLY BILLY"–Probably his name is Billy. Has a habit of saying "Billy Billy" like he's talking to hisself. Like, "Billy Billy, what have you done?" "Billy Billy, got to get the money soon."

"MONEYBAGS"–This woman I don't know where she's from, she always comes in with like wrinkled, greasy money, all tattered ones and fives, like she's never had a clean ten-dollar bill in her life. They say she's got a thin neck, and on her neck over the collarbone there's a tattoo of something in Chinese.

"OLD MISS YOUNG"–Says she's twenty-three. All business, doesn't trick as far as we know, and keeps her private life to herself. Not chatty. Often wears hair-bands with silk flowers or ribbons in them, wears skirts, but she's gawky with knobby knees and looks like she's forty-eight.

"CANCER"–An old black lady with kind of an unhealthy whitish look like her face been dusted with flour, maybe makeup powder. Walks real slow and winces, holding her belly. Says she got a tumor that can't be operated on. Comes dope shopping every fourteen days regular, and usually hooks herself up with a bag of greens and onions from the supermarket on the way home.

That's the best I can do to describe the ones I don't know by name. You can try to spook them out of shopping if you want. But if you have a heart, maybe you'll let them continue to self-medicate. What's there to salvage from these fuck-ups, anyway?

43.

"I GOT a little movement going on inside, you know?"

Efrem had a kind of new rhythm in his speech. His words were nearly the same, and his character had a little bit of the familiar from when we were in juvie together. There was a kind of difference too, like he was kind of interfacing between different cultures.

"There's fourteen of us including me and Nap. We got a pretty secure situation going on. Niggers get bored, though, you know? We don't encourage the boys to get too rowdy, but in the early days we had to fuck some niggers up. Now we just gotta, you know, respect ourselves. We got an anti-narcotics policy, and celibacy is practiced pretty stringently. Maybe our code's not identical to what it was on the street. Seriously, though, it's hard not to see you. And then... it's hard to see you. When I don't see you or the boys for a long time, I get to feeling like I'm nowhere, man."

"I know it. I wish I came out to see you more."

"And when I *do* see you, I'm even more nowhere. Fuck, this is dragging on like a motherfucker. I mean, it ain't all bad. But fuck. I got envy for you."

"Right now we're in a kind of peace and prosperity mode, so it's all cool with us. How's Heaven doing?" I asked.

"Since he got shifted to Wauneka he done put together his own seven-man S·M·F faction. We been wanting to coordinate with you because two of his boys are getting ready to come out soon."

"We'll figure all that out, but how selective are you being?"

"Very."

"Good, because you know Jonas isn't going to want to hear about any boys running around calling theyselves S·M·F while they shitting all over our code."

"Well, when I say 'very selective,' I mean within the scope

of what's possible. These boys in here want some pride and empowerment. But they don't got any notion of societal betterment. I mean, they selfish by nature."

"You indoctrinating them?"

"Yeah, sure. They get it conceptually. We like smart boys as well as strong. But they talk one way and act another."

"Just keep them apprised of the fact we've broken the backs of several sets on the street. We're all of one mind, and we're ready to uphold you as our representative inside. You're getting recognized with O.G. status. Anyone inside or out who don't stay within the law is going to answer for it."

"That's the way it ought to be."

"Just don't let it go to your head."

"Shit, why not? Something's gotta occupy my mind. Why not my extraordinary status and influence?"

"You maintaining any contacts with the Association?"

"Nah. There's no crossing the color line in here."

"What about Los Assesinos."

"They respectful. But distant. Thing is, we don't have any common interests, which makes us useless to them and non-threatening. It's a security in itself. But we like fighting monks, you know? The only fun we got that don't involve knocking a motherfucker around is playing cards. Some boys play chess or dominoes."

"What you need you ain't got?"

"Besides money? Porn. Whatever you can get to us. And pubic hair. We can make a trade with that. Make sure every S·M·F girlfriend and ho makes a contribution. Gotta be real girls. You try to pass off faggot shit, that don't fly."

44.

WE REALLY DID have a period of peace and prosperity. We got back to the little pleasures of life. There was reported to be a citywide decline in gun violence, and I think that was especially true in our area. That was a victory for Jonas and his way. All the clicks were self-policing, looking to maintain business and amicable relations without raising any unnecessary static. Most gangsters were older and more mature now because there was less youth-recruitment going on. In our click, retirees were free to go—but who wants to go when times are easy? And we had a solid enough grip on things that younger sets weren't sprouting up or contesting us.

That don't count Walden Street. They were still punks, and not so well known in terms of they behavior. They were reputed to be armed up with weapons bought off La Fuerza. And they influence was showing itself in new ways. On Rose Street, some crooked landlords pushed out some of the Latin residents by jacking up the rent after "renovating" in a superficial manner, then lowered the rent again in a few months but took only white applications. They wouldn't have dared do that shit without someone backing them.

Jimmy Pricer took off his cloak of invisibility once to stalk around, just to create a scare. "I'm going to kill again," he told some young black kids out playing with they friends. Or so the story was told. It was repeated via Carthage Street.

"He's just selling wolf tickets," said Jonas, and he was right. We tried to contrive a way to get at Pricer and pay him back for the evil he done, but he disappeared as soon as we were looking.

His boys, on they own, got in a minor scuffle with Carthage Lubbs out in no-man's land. They went home from that with bloody noses, fat lips, and tears in they eyes. Nobody dared pull a gat no more.

As for us, we had no further beef to cook. Well... There was one awkward moment I remember when we had to do some conflict resolution, and it didn't have nothing to do with any of our boys. A guy named Paco Ruiz approached us to talk a little business, and Thayne dealt with him on the click's behalf.

As Thayne told it later, Ruiz was complaining a kid from our count had been rude and crossed well over into Los Asesinos territory, where he insulted a girl-cousin of the Gandaras. When he got caught, he told he was protected by the S·M·F.

Thayne said, "He said, 'You know who I am?' he said. 'You, you, you gotta...' he stuttered, and was like, 'Cloud's not going to stand for this. You gotta let me go.' And they were like, 'And who you?' 'Apparel,' he says. 'They call me Apparel.'"

"Apparel?" I asked.

"Yeah. And they say they let the bitch go after some slaps and kicks, but they got his real name out of the cousin—she says he's Leonardo Coleman."

"Leonardo Coleman. I heard that name. Fuck."

"Yeah, it's that kid we chased off once who always acts like he's something. But I told Paco, say, 'I don't know who this Leonardo Coleman is—he sounds like some punk civilian stirring up shit—but we'll find him. He really represented like he was us!?' I asked. 'Fuck,' I said, 'if we gotta discipline him, we'll get him seriously in line and give him the scare of death, but it'd be better you kill him yourself. But we gotta have an agreement, you don't kill him in his house or on our streets. We'll deliver him up, and you pull the trigger.' 'That'd be perfect,' says Paco."

So after talking it over with Jonas and working out a plan, we got Ponder to tell "Apparel" he was going to teach him some car thieving techniques, and maybe if he did a good job we'd buy a car off him. Which is stupid because we never did shit like that, we weren't in the *buying* business, but chumps is chumps. Ponder took him to a quiet suburban street well out of town, to give him a "challenge."

"See how many cars you can slim-jim in five minutes, and see if there's any valuables in the glove compartment. I'll be watching from down the block. If you do good, I'll teach you how to pull an ignition."

While Coleman was working on his first car, a sniper put a bullet through his skull and he was through.

Kid got hisself killed over some stupid shit, and he did it to hisself.

That incident had the added bonus of keeping us on the good side of Los Asesinos and re-cementing our relationship.

Besides that, all was good fun.

Jonas got one of those round swimming pools with the flat bottom and put it on the roof of his house. It probably wasn't so smart to put it there because it took so long to fill with a hose, and the hose had low pressure. Plus we had to drain the pool and clean it several times because we fucked so many women up there no one wanted to swim in the soup. It had the additional disadvantage we had to surround the roof with potted plants to keep the neighbors from spying. But all in all it was good times.

We looked for ways, from time to time, to give the boys new recreational opportunities in between jobs—keep up everyone's spirits. Horseback, now quartermastor since Amazin's disappearance, got approval to spend extra funds on various outings. He had to organize things carefully so everyone felt they got fairly treated, but he worked it out.

For the first time in my life, I got to go on a trip out of town that wasn't strictly for business purposes, and I led an outing to Vegas. We did all kinds of crazy shit on the way out, including seeing a rodeo. It was weird seeing white boys jumping off horses and throwing ropes and shit, but it was a lot more fun and wild than I'd imagined. I think if I was reborn white, well outside the city, I'd spend a lot of time at these kinds of things, whooping it up with Bessie-Mae and drinking plenty of corn liquor.

I got my chance to gamble in Vegas too, recreationally, not with the click's money. It went alright, I made some money, not much—it didn't have any thrill whatsoever, though. Then I went with President for a Grand Canyon helicopter flight. That was fucking insane and I'll never do anything like it again. When we were near the city, I was chill and relaxed, but when we went out further, it was just dreadful. Over the Hoover Dam, I felt really alienated.

When we landed in the canyon to walk around, and we got away from the pilot, I said to President:

"Where do I fit in this environment? Just... what is this?"

"This is nature. Didn't you know?"

"No, I mean, I knew the world is big, but... I feel like I just got swallowed up. Like I don't belong here at all."

"Don't freak out on me."

"I'm just saying this is not a comfortable situation."

I could see he didn't understand my point of view, and when the other boys took they turns they acted all disaffected like this was normal to them. How?

At the end of the trip, Flower made a confession. He was leaving.

"My uncle, he got a new business. I'll be in Arizona helping him to manage it."

"You're kidding. We can't lose you. What are we going to do without you?"

"Good luck."

"What kind of business?"

"He's got a new garage with a partner."

"Arizona? That's crazy."

"We gotta go where life takes us."

"We're going to miss you, seriously. I can't even imagine."

That was a heartbreaker, but, you know, he was one that got out alive.

For the rest of us captains and O.G.s it was back to the grind, and for the younger soldiers it was new ropes and new adventures. But without much fighting going on, I think the younger guys' puffed up bravado was mostly a front at this point. It's a paradox. We love the good times, but we never know when too much good will make us too soft to survive the next battle.

45.

JONAS HAD a nine-year-old son.

If telling it to you like this seems abrupt, maybe you can imagine how I felt when I found out.

Fierce saw Jonas driving downtown with the top of his car down and a little kid sitting in the passenger seat. He told it to me, I told Lettuce, and together we waited to ambush Jonas at the clubhouse. We had time for some refreshment while we waited.

"What the fuck!?" we shouted when he finally came in.

"Whoah! What the fuck yourselves!?"

"Jonas, what's going on?"

"We heard you had some kid in your car. You giving tours to underprivileged kids or something?"

"Hoah... Wait, wait up."

"What's up?"

"Who saw me?"

"I did," said Fierce. "But maybe not just me. You can't ride around town and think you won't be recognized."

"Listen... You're talking about my son."

"Son!?"

"What!?"

"How you have a son?"

"That's a big infant!"

"Yeah, he's big. Listen. I didn't even know I had a kid until very, very recently. His mom never told me. I ain't even seen her for so long."

"How old is he?"

"Nine."

"Whoaaaaaaaahh!"

"Alright, that's crazy, Jonas. When'd you find out?"

"Like, eight months ago."

"Eight months!?"

"That's a long time to sit on a secret like that."

"I don't want everyone knowing, you know. My life... I tell you everything. But this one thing is a big deal. I don't need everyone to know."

"Damn right, it's a big deal. It's dangerous."

"You know what Sammy would say if he was here?" said Fierce.

"What?"

"You are fathor!"

Almost like a magic cue, Sammy walked right in the door that exact moment:

"You are fathor!!" he proclaimed.

"... and he do appear!"

"What are we talking about?" Sammy asked.

"Jonas has a kid."

"What? You mean I wasn't just joking when I said that?"

"Where'd you come from?"

"I heard you kids laughing. I just came in from the car. Cloud gave me a ride."

"And he didn't even tell you where he was just before he picked you up?"

"What's the kid's moniker?" I asked.

"He's not going to have anything to do with gang life."

"I think we should call him 'Little Cloud'," said Sammy.

"You're not going to see him. I'm not bringing him around you. You all bad role models."

"And who taught us to be that way?"

"My son's name is Philip."

"You named him after me?" asked Lettuce. "I'm flattered."

"No, I didn't name him. His mom did."

"Philip Dandridge? That's a classy name."

"I don't know that he uses Dandridge. I think he uses his mom's mom's name. Which I'm not repeating here because it's none of your fucking business."

"Dude, you know like how many times I jerk it in a week, and you think it's too personal to admit to fatherhood?"

"Kid looked white too," said Fierce.

"Now hold on! You can't be talking about his appearance like that."

"I'm not saying anything negative. He's a handsome boy. But he looked a little... pale. Don't he?"

"Now it's time to just move on to another conversation."

"Hoah...! Is his mom white?"

"She might be."

"Oh my God. It's a racial revolution."

"That's enough. Screw down."

"I..."

Jonas raised his finger to silence Sammy's next words.

"This knowledge goes in the crypt. Not a one of you speaks of it."

"Too late," said Sammy.

"Why? You only heard of it this minute."

"That don't matter. Once a secret goes beyond one person, everyone knows. We don't even gotta talk. It goes out by osmosis."

We all laughed.

"That's good."

"Serious, though. There's no such thing as a secret between five people. Six? There's the kid too. And his mom?"

"You might as well tell everyone," I said, "because I don't want everyone coming back recriminating each other, 'You told it,' 'I told it.' It's out."

"Shit," said Jonas. He dropped onto a sofa looking really distressed. "Yeah."

"Kid's got forty-four uncles!"

"Ha!"

"Lid off, bitches," said Jonas. "Might as well tap in the whiskey reserves. We'll have a party for the announcement, but I'm telling you, I'm not bringing Philip around any of you. Not once, not never."

"We'll call that a reasonable compromise. I never introduced you to my pet hamster either."

46.

WHEN NEW YEARS came around, we received a case of rum shipped up from Barbados. Trice had retired after all. It came with a note:

"I had a cop-killer friend committed suicide in prison. I realized, 'What the fuck am I doing here?' Six months back from exile and I was jaded and sick of it all, so I'm out. Now another ambitious young fool has the keys, and if you want my advice you'll continue to honor our pact, but you won't do any further trusting with regards to the new crew. But if y'all are ever down in the Caribbean some time, well... Red Green might point you in the right direction if you ask him nice. Happy New Year."

47.

IT KIND OF DISTURBED ME one day when I went up on the roof of Jonas's place when there was no one around. I came out the door to the roof, and I saw the dark back heel of a leather shoe and the black top of an open umbrella disappearing around the corner past the side wall of the stairwell. I went around to see who it was. There was no one there. *Could... could someone have jumped off the roof silently?*

I walked to the wall and looked over the edge.

No one and nothing.

That was a strangely specific illusion.

48.

"Why don't you marry the mother of your child?" I asked Jonas.

"She's a good mom. I'm taking care of him and her both. I supply money. I visit sometimes. But, you know, marriage is the death of the gangster."

"True. But maybe you can afford to die."

"Nice thought. Nah, I don't have the money to live on for a lifetime. I treat the click well, as you know. I ain't broke, but I ain't set for forty years, and I don't think I ever will be."

"How many kids you know our age who's set to live without ever working they whole lives?"

"So what am I going to do?"

"You could do something, I'm sure. You talented like anyone."

He gave a bitter laugh to this. "Anyway, I don't expect there to be anything when this all plays out. I got my mission. I got my place to be as long as there's an S·M·F to back me up."

"Faithful to your boys always, I know. But you got someone else to look out for now."

"From a distance."

"You're not going to dirty him."

Another laugh. "Shit, I can't even touch his mom now, hardly. Most of the time I visit, I just hand over the cash, smile, give the boy a toy or two, and play the hero."

"You're too constrained when, you know, you're the freest of us all. And there's not a person but you to hold you to anything."

"I know where I stand. I'm down to zero outs, but that's alright with me. There's never going to be an 'after' as far as my life and the click is concerned. Anyway, what's going on? You jockeying to take my place?"

"You know I wouldn't."

"Yeah, I know."

49.

WHILE HE WAS hanging with some girl at a park across town, Slice got shot at by some unidentified person.

"I got shot at," he said.

"And?"

"I dodged."

"It happens. Never mind it."

"Who did it?"

"Doesn't matter. We're not going to war over getting shot *at*."

Hostility lurks around corners. Sometimes the unknown catches us unawares.

50.

Time rolled, money flowed, humans paid what humans owed.

Although we continued to have our little dramas now and then—we had to deal with some of our boys getting locked up for short to medium spells when thefts went wrong—we started to get a lot of our entertainment from the news and gossip that was spreading from neighborhoods around us.

No one heard from Carthage street in months. The Lubbs did so little to catch our notice, it took us a long time to recognize they dissolved. Poof, gone.

It was this new kid rose up, a guy named Darwin Mister, nicknamed Hellish, who took over the local business by virtue of being more violent and confrontational than the Lubbs he displaced. He ran out they leaders and they folded. His set wasn't very formally organized so they got known just as Darwin's Crew. When we heard about it, Jonas wanted to call Hellish in for a confab. Hardcore went to set it up.

Hardcore came back and said to Jonas, "He got significant respect for you. S·M·F too. So he'll meet if you come to him. But he's got that paranoid edge, you know. He's not straying out his count right now."

"Nah. You go, Brain. Be our voice and sort shit out."

So it was up to me. Hardcore came along, and I brought Fierce too so he could get diplomacy experience.

Hellish met us in his shorts and a wife-beater, smoking a joint in his house. No one was in but him, which was weird, especially for a so-called paranoid. What did he have to protect him? It was like he was flaunting his carelessness when we thought he'd try to display his strength.

"How'd I guess Cloud would never come out here hisself."

"There's nothing Cloud *wouldn't* do. He's got his will, you know?"

"That's fine."

"You got any kin in the neighborhood?"

"Sure. Not in the house right now, though."

"Brothers?"

"You don't know shit about me, do you?"

"No."

"My brother got killed."

It was hard to relax here because he wasn't offering us anything to drink or anything. We smoked tobacco while he smoked weed. And he looked from one to another of us.

"Shit, I know all about you, though," he said. Then he addressed me in particular. "I heard you're closer to Cloud than anyone."

I turned to Fierce, laughed, and said, "Don't tell Thayne he said that." Then I thought, *Why Thayne? Why I didn't think of President or Lettuce before Thayne?* Hell. I knew it was true, though, that Thayne might be the only one that would be jealous.

"Listen," said Darwin, "It's weird, though, you coming here. Is this a show of force?"

"No force. We came here weak, man. Only three of us."

"Hell, if I had three killers like you though, I could do shit. Not like I ain't did shit. I got the whole of Carthage. I own it. You ain't never come out and see the Family of Man, though."

"We didn't get on with them."

"Me neither. I took them apart."

"Who? How?"

"Wadud was the first."

"Never heard of him."

"Well, he dead."

"You sure he's dead? We ain't heard of it."

"Am I sure? Well, I don't know. If he can survive a bullet in the brain and another in the heart, good luck to him."

Hardcore laughed. "Shit, you're funny, dude."

"We ain't heard about that."

"You don't hear about everything. Why you come here anyway? Do we have any common interests?"

"Our interests are always growing."

"Heh. That sounds like a threat, but I don't listen. It's good to see you and look you in the eyes—know what I'm dealing with on a more personal level..."

I had a vision then in my mind that things were going to go wrong—maybe Darwin was going to have to die. I don't know why I thought that. I felt he was going to say some shit that'd make that happen, and I had to stop it before it came to that.

"Shut up. Sorry, but I don't want to hear you say something that takes it..."

"You're in my house..."

"That's why I'm doing you the courtesy..."

The rest of what we said didn't make much sense, but I let him know to keep his shit constrained, and then we got out of there and avoided a more outrageous scene. I don't know who was more confused by the whole fallout of this dialog, him or us.

Outside, before we climbed in my personal Caddy, I saw, across the street, a car that hadn't been there before, with three boys in it watching the house and us.

We drove off.

"How'd it go?" Jonas asked when we returned.

"It went well. We're cool with Mister. He knows his place."

"But..."

"I told him his place, man. Now, chill."

Jonas had his own parley with Darwin a few days after that, but I didn't get invited along and I don't know what they said.

Strange things were going on. A crazy white boy from south of Yost came and burned some trees in Brandywine Park on a midday. Said he wanted to send a message. No one knew what his message was. The cops took him away.

❧

Another crazy thing. A big one.

A star player on the basketball team at Liberty High School in South Brehms—another white boy—created a scandal when he shot and killed his girlfriend.

"Dude was a Walden Street Boy. Ricky Wilson."

"Hey, he pretty big with them."

"Yeah, but people out they mind, man. Can you believe he fucked it all up just to get some secret dick?"

"Huh?"

"You didn't hear that? His girl told everyone about a time she and Ricky had sex with a dude. Ricky gave the guy a blowjob, and with that story going around causing so much scandal, he killed the bitch for outing him as a bisexual."

"Damn, they problems go deep."

"That's the stupidest reason to kill I ever heard," said Sammy. "I mean, if you don't want to be known as a guy who sucks dicks, fine, the solution is simple. Don't suck dicks. But if you want to do that, why be ashamed?"

"Whoah, Sammy, come on!"

"I mean, you know how many dicks there are in the world? Someone's gotta suck them."

"Sammy, fuck you, come on," said Flip. "Gay is gay."

"Is that in the rulebook, Cloud? Gay is gay?"

"I think that don't need to be written down," said Flip.

"You do know what we grooming you for, right?"

This nearly lead to some violence, but I restored order. There was no sense Flip getting offended by a joke.

But the Ricky Wilson thing was serious. When cops searched his home in pursuance of the murder case, they turned up some product and some evidence linking him to Joseph Sharp, Pricer's deputy. Lord Jimmy Pricer was now in permanent hiding, and as some older whites were getting tired of aligning theyselves with a bunch of young punk thugs who did more to terrorize they own neighborhood than protect it, shit was starting to really come apart for Walden Street.

Los Asesinos pounced. They stepped in and claimed Rose Street for theyselves. They came out of nowhere and moved to intimidate some Walden Street Boys congregated in a Rose Street lot, and when the Boys wouldn't stand down, there was a non-fatal shooting of one soldier. Unfortunately, the shooter got identified, caught, and jailed. But they got a solid hold on the street.

Los Asesinos weren't committed to taking the fight much further. They got what they came for. They put some pressure on the offending landlords who'd been working to keep the street white, and rumor said the landlords started paying them protection money. But the tenant policy didn't seem to change. Honestly, I don't know.

❧

Another interesting development was when someone found a skeleton buried in a vacant lot was getting built up into a playground in Jack-Rabbit Corner. Police found jewelry, a rotten old wallet with decayed papers, and they looked at the corpse's teeth. Somehow they used that for an I.D.—police must have had a hunch. Turned out it was Leeshawn Levant, the old Jack-Rabbit F.O.M. chief.

"Wow. I thought for sure he'd run. And here he was dead all along."

We had a laugh about that.

Police had suspicion on us, but we hadn't done it, and it came to nothing. It didn't hurt our image in the community, though, to have that killing attributed to us.

"You know, they could by lying about the I.D.," said Sammy. "You think that fucker even went to the dentist?"

51.

ACE, HARDCORE, FORTRESS, Bank, and I were out doing rounds outside of the count, collecting from some of the debtors who'd fallen behind. We were dragging with us one baby named Mike who might make soldier soon. We met with the usual frustrations with our customers, but we squeezed the money out of them mostly, with apologies and promises from two who were just unable to cough up.

Halfway through our rounds, we took a break, got out our cars, and walked to stretch our legs. Mike wanted to show he wasn't afraid to use his mouth, so he opened up talking about, "I heard there's this La Fuerza kid just made his seventh kill last week, and the police won't touch him."

Hardcore took the opportunity to straighten this kid out, let him know where we stand, and pass on a war-story about a soldier who'd lately got killed. He gave due credit to Solid, one of our finest.

"Man, boys out here always talking like they did shit. Seen shit. Everyone's tellin' they stories, you know. Half those stories don't mean nothing. Kids are full of theyselves, always trying to build theyselves up, you know. Don't listen to any of that. You got the boys over in the other clicks talkin' about how many bodies they got, right? All boastful and shit. Then you gotta look at like a guy like Solid, right? You ever hear him boast about anything? He's a quiet guy, you know? Humble. But, you know, maybe his pride is in his bearing, you know, not in his words. Solid, man, he's seen more shit than half those boys out there. I'm telling you. Fortress, he tell you about Smooch?"

"Yeah, yeah, yeah. That boy who, uh, got killed, right? Fell out a window."

"Yeah, fell out a window, sure. Got pushed out a window." He turns back to the kid. "Solid was taking Smooch around like we showing you. Smooch had to start learning how to collect, right, you know? So he goes and plays rough with a debtor, you know, trying to get the guy cough up the money. Pushed too hard, I guess. Debtor pushed him back, pushed him right out the window. You know, Solid was right outside, he hears a noise and comes running. What do you think he sees, right up on that paling of that iron fence, right outside the building?"

"What?"

"There's Smooch's head, right, stuck right on there. Like a pumpkin or something with a skewer in it. And what's there slouched, down on the ground? Well, there's the rest of him. His body's lying there, looking almost relaxed like, *Oops, forgot to bring my head!* Telling you, seeing something like that, shake you up, right? Solid, he ever talk about that? He don't talk about that. You know, he's seen a lot of shit, done a lot of shit. But he don't talk about shit. Not out there always boasting. Boys out there, boasting, they act like they got something to talk about. Solid, you know, all he gotta do is walk someplace, or drive someplace, boys look at him like, Damn, that boy is serious!"

"Yeah, but what happened to the debtor, huh? The guy who pushed Smooch, huh?"

"Uh, you know, Solid ain't tell the rest of the story. He took care of it, you know. That's what I'm saying, you know. There's one guy dead, Solid tells the story, he don't talk about that. He don't gotta talk about that. He don't gotta build a reputation on what he's done, you know. He just done it. You know, even faced by something serious—tsk—he just takes care of business."

Along the way we stopped for hotdogs.

"These dogs are good."

"Nah, they alright."

"No, these are good. Why can't we get something like this near us?"

"We eat good food at the barbecues."

"Yeah, but I mean on a daily basis."

"What are you fussing about? You don't eat?"

"I eat."

"There's Pete's on Silver."

"But they suck. What is that? They boil the hotdogs in a vat with old socks or something?"

"We got oxtail and jerk chicken up at Zion…"

"I like the macaroons at Rainbow."

"I told you, that's not the point. I eat. I'm just saying I like *this*. Why can't we get *this*?"

"You must be hungry today or something. Damn. I never heard anybody talk about a hotdog with such enthusiasm."

We were walking along the sidewalk close to the curb. A mid-sized white truck rolled by, not too fast, also close to the curb. When it had almost passed him by, Ace, who was lagging a little behind, stuck his foot out under the rear wheel so the top of his foot was broken, the heel was pressed hard against the curbstone, and his ankle twisted and snapped. He fell in agony. I only saw because I was turning to talk.

"Aaaah!!"

"What happened?"

"Why'd you do that!?" I asked.

"My foot's broken! Aaahhh!" He was on his ass, gripping the mauled foot.

"Why?"

The truck stopped, and as we turned, I saw now the driver looking at our reflection in his sideview mirror. Then he drove off.

"It fucking ran over my foot!"

"Ace, what the fuck!?"

"Did anyone see the license?"

"Shit. Run up the block."

"4753. I don't know, there was some letters."

"Oh God! I can't walk!"

"Why did you do that?"

"It was the truck."

"I know, but you stuck your foot out."

"I don't know why. Seriously, I just don't know. I thought about doing it, and then I did it."

A serious psych case in our click. We had to drum him out. Who knows what kind of situation Ace would have landed us in if he broke down during a job or in the middle of a fight—or could he even turn violent against a brother? Who knows? And he was with us from the beginning. The very beginning. It was sick. It was pathetic. A lot of us talked about it. We had a lot of love for Ace, but we couldn't understand what had become of him.

52.

JUST WHEN JONAS was getting curious again—just when we were seeking out new ways to get at Pricer again, to have another go at killing him—we found out we missed our opportunity, permanently. The cops surprised everyone by actually doing they job. Pricer was arrested for murder.

They couldn't connect him to the lynchings. They said there wasn't evidence to get them on that. But they did bust him for killing John Covington in New Mexico, the first kill he claimed.

What they had, according to reports, was a newly cooperative witness, an ex-girlfriend of Covington who says she was in the house when it happened. There was some bloodied clothing, sheets, blankets cops had gathered from the crime scene, and now they had a recovered weapon the girl led them to, with ballistics reports and fingerprints. It was a solid case when the parts came together. The official story didn't say anything about a duel—what a bullshit story!—and the prosecutor didn't name a motive for the crime. The victim was found shot through the side of the head, probably killed while sitting on the edge of his bed—probably caught by surprise.

Cops picked up Pricer in a suburban home where he was living just then with a middle-aged white lady, supplier of product to the Walden Street Boys and several other crews. Pricer had business in other neighborhoods we never heard of. The bitch was taken in on drug charges and pressured to testify. In the end, Pricer's wrinkly old lover-slash-sugar-mama turned witness on him.

Cool he went down. Not so cool he dodged us.

So I was all mixed up by this crazy turn. This here, now, if you want to know the truth, is the point in the narrative where, if I had been generol of the S·M·F, it would have all come apart. We were right there at the peak of our influence—or nearly there—and our chief boogeyman was taken and locked away, no one was giving us any grief, yet all I could see when I heard this news was a slow slide into oblivion. Jonas, though, he held it together. For a while.

53.

THE QUALITY of the food we ate was getting better and better to the point we got snobby about it. There was a short-lived red-wine trend, but that was just playing. We had contrary obligations. Jonas discouraged us from spending too much on one bottle, but on the other hand, we wouldn't be allowed to go and get wasted too often on Carlo by the jug. We had to have class without ostentation, and falling out your pants with long strings of drool to the concrete was frowned upon.

Secretly, I liked to buy a fifty dollar Gigondas from time to time, which I still maintain is a good bottle for a man. It wasn't that secret, though, since I sometimes shared with Jonas. His main thing was not to give the wrong impression to the troops.

I still think sometimes what most people can't get is that the good life is sometimes good in itself, and it can't be measured in dollars spent. I remember holding forth on this one time at a casual party while I was slightly zoned. Some younger soldiers were getting a bit of my teacherness.

"Raw pleasure—even kids can understand that—and then there's a kind of flash that dazzles the eyes. But I think it takes years of luxury, sometimes, until you learn to calm the fuck down so you can appreciate things. It's like progress back to the basic, you know? And when you live a fast life, how can that even happen? But I hope someday I can reach a state of mind where I can even find appreciation for the crude again—recapture that happiness I didn't know was once mine because I was just running past it in my youth—and now I'll have a more profound contentment such that with even nothing I can be satisfied. Or maybe I'll understand it's something different—like we just get flashes of happiness between the ordinary times—and you just gotta receive them."

"Dude needs to shut up," said Sammy. "Who he think he is, E.F. Hutton?"

He always trumped me in the wisdom game.

54.

AND HERE'S WHERE shit snapped. The last vestiges of the Walden Street Boys went crazy. They took they energy, they hunger, they humiliated pride, and they channeled it all into a conflict with Darwin's Crew on Carthage. The battle was hot, bullets were flying, civilians were back to hiding in they homes and walking with stooped shoulders whenever they had to go out for beer, drugs, or education.

"Where'd they find they heart all of a sudden?" said president at one of our meetings.

"They despairing, you know?" said Lettuce. "You can't put down a desperate man."

"Nah, that's nonsense," said Thayne. "Humans can always be worse crushed. When the will is sufficiently shattered, there's no resistance."

"Well, they ain't reached that kind of breaking point," I said. "They fighting."

"This is where lives get cheap, though, man," said Lettuce. "They fighting for crumbs. Between they two sets, maybe they got a couple hundred addicts to cater to. That's only a few hundred thousand dollars. You can't feed many soldiers on that. Especially if you gotta arm them too."

"Shylock's got it all in his account book," said Sammy.

For all the madness that went on, it took a week before anyone died. The Walden Street Boys scored a kill against Darwin's Crew. A soldier named Warren Cherry got pinned down in an alley off Osbourne while the rest of his boys got driven off by heavy gunfire. Walden Street Boys couldn't drive him out, so they rushed him en masse, at serious risk, but they got him.

Two weeks later, Darwin and his boys went to the funeral of they fallen brother. Jonas sent me and Hardcore to show our sympathies. I wish he hadn't, so I wouldn't have had to witness the carnage.

White boys rushed the cemetery in the middle of everything and shot and killed Darwin, surrounded by his set.

I turned into a rubbery, blubbery idiot.

They wounded civilian mourners, including one old aunt of the boy in the casket. Everyone scattered, lay out on the ground with they heads in they hands, or hid behind tombs and monuments. The shooters vanished.

Hardcore and I screamed bloody murder at Jonas back at the clubhouse about what the hell could we do about this. It wasn't even one of us that died.

S·M·F twiddled our thumbs while some boys from Carthage went up and, unable to find any Walden Street Boys in the open, they shot into random homes up and down the street.

Police were all over everything. Every neighborhood around, including ours, got quiet and cautious. The indecency of murder at a funeral, in the midst of the victim's kin...

The skull opens up and the darkness pours out.

❧

Jonas kept us calm while he sought and found a way we could capitalize.

In the days that followed, Jonas was out on Carthage Street acting like it was our part of town, filling Darwin's vacuum, and he was talking to everyone he could meet. He was out of his car, talking to strangers, talking to kin of the Lubbs that went dormant, and also to Darwin's boys. Far from acting like an outsider, he was playing like he was just elected the new mayor.

Cops tried to talk to Darwin's relatives, and nobody said to keep it quiet. Kin's got the right to seek justice wherever they can find it, I guess, when things get as bad as this.

And I was out there by Jonas's side sometimes, trying to talk some sense into him. One day, a detective walked out on the street coming out the Misters's house. He got a few looks from the neighbors. Everyone kind of hung back and wouldn't approach, while he looked searching for someone in the crowd that might be sympathetic. Our thought was, *Is he really going to help, or is this just another job to him?* None of us trusted him, but it was like, *Fuck, is there a way out?* Jonas then walked up and shook the detective's hand.

"We gotta do something about this, really," said Jonas.

"I know we do," said the cop. "We are doing absolutely everything we can to restore some security…"

"There's never been any security here. But you gotta look at root causes of this. The racial causes, and the breakdown, you know… what's brought about by lack of hope."

The detective looked like, *What the hell is this, some kind of politics?* He made polite parting remarks and retreated to his car to get the hell out of dodge.

I just got this shock, like, *He's not going to ask any questions? Jonas gave him this surprise opening, and now he don't want to hear it? Really? That wouldn't happen, right?*

Jonas was out there daily, showing his face, trying to boost up morale. There was no concrete action, just talk. To him he was building community relations. And he was out there nightly too. Unarmed, always. If we O.G.s wanted to accompany, he sometimes let us, but then he got tired of us looking like bodyguards and distancing him from humans. If we didn't go, he went alone. He made hisself an emblem of fearless self-confidence, there on Carthage and anywhere else. He could have got shot at any time, murdered from any angle. He was telling humans, "Come out. Walk. Remember these are your streets." And some were listening—not just gangsters, but moms, uncles, and kids who didn't normally show theyselves without some kind of encouragement. Local drug trade really got froze up for a while.

He also walked up and down Walden Street one night alone. And the next night too. Really putting a thumb in they eye now. The so-called courageous Walden Street Boys. Not terrorizable, some had said. But he didn't prompt a reaction.

Finally, we grabbed Jonas and kept him home. There's only so much crazy we can let our generol get away with before it looks like an explicit suicide attempt.

He still staged one more stunt, though. A big one.

Weeks went by until arrangements had been made for Darwin Mister's funeral, the coroner had finished investigating his body and taking evidence for the ongoing investigation, yada, yada. The Mister clan was worried there'd be new violence at the funeral, and it wasn't expected many people would attend because even some who were closest to him might be afraid to show, or some would be embarrassed by the spectacle. But Jonas talked to everyone and arranged a convoy of cars driven by our captains—and a few soldiers who had cars—and offered rides to everyone in the neighborhood who wanted to go. He managed to assemble quite a crowd, preaching how important it was to honor the dead and not stand for injustice.

A truce was sworn between the leftovers of the Lubbs and Darwin's remaining Crew. We did what we could to make it hold.

Jonas's scheme was to tie in the funeral to a protest march he arranged on Walden Street, as a show of force and moral strength.

55.

THE HEARSE PULLED UP at the intersection of Belle Isle and Walden. I, Thayne, President, and Lettuce got out to serve as pall bearers. We lifted the heavy—and expensive!—cherry-wood casket, and headed the procession, with Jonas walking beside us. The hearse followed, with the string of cars trailing along, and we were accompanied by crowds of supporters.

"No more violence! No more violence!" humans were chanting as we marched. Several locals were out on they stoops to watch us, or watched from upper-story windows. There were maybe only a few minority residents in the area, but all were out, or anyway most of them.

Jonas was shouting messages along the way. "It's time for justice!" "We have to bring this warfare to a close!" "Too many have died!" "We will take order in our own hands!" There was a stream of messages. I'm not sure they jibed with each other, but crowd response was positive. Meanwhile we were sweating, lugging, and looking sad like we ought to.

Only one brave soul dared to confront us. He came out his front door and stood on the stoop, shirtless. A young man.

"Take your nigger tears to the cemetery!" he shouted.

Some of the crowd rushed up on his stoop, and he ran in and locked his door. We made note of the address. Jonas did his best to call off the mob before they gave the guy a pretext to shoot us.

"Don't get baited by hateful words. Today, we rise above that. Keep marching. For Darwin!"

When we'd walked to Ridge Avenue, we stopped and put the casket back in the hearse. The convoy drove on while Jonas paused to address his final comments to the pedestrian crowd.

"Disunity is what made us vulnerable, but standing together is where we'll find our strength. There will be no more tolerance for brother fighting brother—not in this part of town.

So me and my brothers, we're going show you how to keep it together and keep our heads high."

The cars and most of the marchers went on to the funeral, but the hearse that led the way made a detour. As you may have guessed, there wasn't a body in the box. The Mister family wasn't going to agree to have they son used that way, and they didn't take part in our protest. But we'd made our point, and most humans were no wiser to what went on. Our convoy delivered everyone from the neighborhood to the funeral home where the family had already completed a private ceremony for they son. The masses took part in the burial rite, throwing heaps of flowers and parting gifts—some bags of marijuana were among them. The police kept the scene secure, and everything went off very peacefully and respectfully.

You might wonder what happened to our empty but genuine casket. Well, later, that dirty dog Sammy fucked a woman in it. She somehow ripped the silk interior with a high-heel shoe.

"What are we going to do with the casket now?" asked Lettuce.

"Keep it," said Sammy. "You can bury me in that shit when it's my time. Or you can just feed me to the rats. I don't really care."

But after keeping it around for a while as a novelty, we repaired the interior and sold it back into another funeral home. Maybe your grandma's buried in it.

56.

As a sequel to all this, we went back to the house of that Walden Street Boy who heckled us and had a talk with him. He was a captain, one of the last ones standing, a guy named Oscar. We told him to clear out in ten days if he wanted to live. He told us we should pay him compensation for the business they'd lost and the decimation of they crew. We told him his life would be adequate compensation for everything he'd lost, if he only managed to get the hell out and take it with him.

Eight days later he was still hanging around, so we broke him up with bats.

When he got out the hospital, he left town, as did all the rest of the Walden stragglers. That was they demise.

Now, I gotta tell you an interesting truth, and I don't even know what to make of it. If it had been me, I would have come back. I mean, if I was in Oscar's situation, even all broke up, I would have returned. Not now. Since then I've learned a few things. Now I think I'd do just like he did and get out with my life. But back then, when I had the S·M·F still deep in my blood, I would have come back and died rather than run. Brotherhood. That was the foundation of our click's mad strength. I think a lot of us would honestly have done that. Back then.

57.

WE NEVER talked about fear.

Guncracks kept sounding, now and again, here and there. That sound—sometimes it's a chattering of voices from Hell. Sometimes, the bullets, they're the cold truth—a kind of fatalism puts knots in the stomach to think about. You never get used to that noise, really, even when you ignore it, something inside is listening. And for all the years I've put on a mask of fearlessness—unaffectedness—there's a sickening variety of ways hearing gunshots can wear you down. It's a Chinese water-torture.

Yeah, we didn't talk about that. Fear is something we never could talk about.

Complaints, we had. Sometimes regrets. Never weakness.

58.

"I SET OUT to do good, you know?" Back at the bar again with Jonas, one to one. Speaking of regrets. "I just had this crazy notion if I got to him, you know... it felt like it would have meant something..."

"What are you talking about?"

"... but that's stupid. I gotta say, I been lucky all around. Don't get married to a kill. It's no good."

"What kill?"

"Pricer."

"Oh. Him."

"I mean, even righteous anger, that's a distraction. I serve my boys first. S·M·F, that's forever. But to relish something, that's dangerous man, it could be a trap you don't get out of."

"Uh huh."

"Learn it. We're not a means to an end. We're an end. We already got all we want, right here, right now. That's where happiness lies, man."

"I know you wanted that kill, Jonas. You don't gotta convince me. You don't gotta earn our love and respect. You got it every day. From me, for sure, and from every Serious Mother Fucker there is. We've learned."

"Cool. Not that I doubted. Anyway. Think it's time for another party?"

"Summer will be soon."

59.

JONAS WAS at a high point for respect and authority. And I didn't think he could have risen higher than when we swept the Black Steel Nines away and took possession of the corner from the Lubbs. And here he was, master of a larger count than ever, helping to rebuild Darwin's Crew under they new leader, Denny "Meek" Drayton, setting up a vassal state.

We didn't get love from the majority of the whites, but we got reluctant respect and got the chance for a stable count with stable borders while elevating the status of the black families that still resided on Walden and Osbourne. Rose fell permanently to Los Asesinos, which we expected.

Jonas got Bank on the job of identifying some reliable white businessman-wanabes we could lend money to to revitalize the area and draw our share of the profit. In next to no time, one lot got converted to a self-storage facility, and another became a minimart with milk and smokes. We kept our numbers games out of the neighborhood to avoid accusations of corrupting the community, but we gave the local complexion a bit of a tan by forcing the self-storage boss to employ some S·M·F associates for security and night-management positions.

So what was Jonas thinking all this time while things were turning out so well? I felt like I knew him and didn't know him at the same time. I didn't know what would be the next thing to make us all jump. I didn't know what Jonas was going to say or do that might change things overnight. I felt confidence in him and doubt too. Or am I just remembering it that way? It's like, what's more terrifying than holding something precious in your hand and feeling a little... slip? Just imagining it—I don't like imagining it.

I brought in a guy I thought would make a great soldier for us. He had all the heart in the world, he was young and bright, he idolized Cloud. He was awed when he met me. Respectful. And he wanted to give everything to the S·M·F.

I don't need to name him. He didn't get made.

Jonas interviewed him:

"Why do you want to be with us?"

"I... Freedom is my birthright. It will not be taken."

"You don't have to give me a pat answer. Brain's already tested you, now I want to know your true heart."

"Well, the form may be pat, but the meaning is true. I really mean it. I've got... I've got to take what I got, myself, you know, and turn it to a purpose. For the brothers and the community."

"Listen. You seem so fucking smart, I think you got a lot to be proud of. Brain knows a lot of what people are made of. But you want to have a purpose? Hell, go help your mom, your sister, whoever you got. Go help your community, but forget about us."

"Struggling alone is a meaningless life."

"Fuck no. You find meaning... you find meaning somehow. You don't need us, and our work is getting done fine without you. And another thing. S·M·F don't bring an end to your struggles. Only death does that."

"I... I'm not against struggling, it's just about turning it to the right purpose."

"I'm not testing you anymore, man, I'm for real. I reject you. Not because you're not good enough, but because we're not good enough for you."

"But you've... you've made changes in the community, you know, and... listen, I don't care if you're testing me or not, this is what I believe and I want to make my contribution..."

"*Screw* the fuck *down*, alright? Take a gift when it's offered. I'm giving you the true gift, the real freedom. I'm telling you get out... Go!"

I'd seen Jonas reject kids, but somehow never like this.

"What the hell was that?" I asked him.

"Don't play dumb, you heard all I said."

"But why'd you reject him?"

"Take it at face value, Mala, and stop blinding yourself. It's all context, you know. We got no reason to drag him down with us now. If only I'd known years ago..."

He started to walk away mumbling like we were finished with the conversation.

"Fucking philosophy, man," I said. "Today you're in a funk, and tomorrow's another story. It's always fucking like this and I'm sick of it."

60.

THEN THE WORST thing that could happen happened. Jonas got shot while walking with his son Philip—by now I'd forgot the child because so much else was going on all the time, and Jonas never did bring him around. But while the kid was out of my mind, he was clearly never out of Jonas's thoughts.

They came out a shoe store, and someone—we don't know who—lit them up. I wasn't there. One more story had to be pieced together after the fact. The first bullet caught the boy in the face and he died on the spot. Jonas got hit in the chest, abdomen, and jaw. God wasn't merciful that day because Jonas's wounds didn't knock him out. He was incapacitated, but he had time to witness the miserable death of his only child.

It took Jonas six days to die. For the first four days in I.C.U., he was awake for several hours a day, before he went into his final coma.

We took turns visiting him, and I and Sammy and the O.G.s, we were the ones who spent the most time with him. Even though he couldn't move his jaw, and though he had an oxygen mask, Jonas was capable of a little mumbled speech at first, when he tried.

"You don't know, Mala. You don't know," is what he told me. He was thinking of his son, I'm sure.

Toxins spread through his body. Doctors said his organs were failing, the drugs they were administering had not been able to stabilize him, and the process could not be reversed unless his body got its immune system under control. That was unlikely. And Jonas didn't beat the odds.

I think there was no peace in his mind at any time.

I was right by his hospital bed at the end when he died. At that point it was just a quiet fading away, but that wasn't any consolation for the psychic suffering I know he felt up till then. His grandma wasn't there. His mom wasn't there. Sammy? Yeah, he was there.

I'm not trying to present you with a morality tale here, because we didn't learn shit from Jonas's death, and it's something that didn't have to happen. But it happened.

❧

As for all this... I've assembled these memories here because they're all I'm left with. There was so much went on in between the beginning and end of this all that has become vague and uncertain. I reckon it didn't all make sense. But I've shared what I know—what was important—and maybe a little more.

❧

There was a funeral. Goddamn.

At the funeral, Thayne said to me, "I loved and honored Cloud as much as you or anybody else. S·M·F, though, it's changing."

Fucker was geared for business. That's all.

"Change can't be avoided," said I. "Right?" said I.

"That's the way I see it," said he.

❧

Jonas Dandridge... You got it all. He was a great man.

He was only five days older than I, but he was my true father, and I loved him to death.

Book Design

Front-cover photograph by Willi Heidelbach.

Photographs on back cover courtesy The U.S. National Archives, photographed by John H. White.

National archive identifiers:

Decorated Wall: 412-DA-13779

Welders: 412-DA-13815

Typefaces

Book interior, back-cover copy, and "Metarules":

ITC Mendoza font family

Gang name "S·M·F" in cover title:

825Karolus Titling

Author's Name on cover and spine:

ITC Legacy Sans